THE BOOK OF ADVENTURES 2:

THE ADVENTURES OF JAKE AND MASON

GREGORY BOUTHIETTE

PRAISE FOR
THE BOOK OF ADVENTURES 2

"Imagine *The Legend of Zelda* adapted as a British sitcom, jam-packed with brilliant deadpan humor and wonderful adventure. This book is fun as hell."
> —Max Booth III, author of *The Nightly Disease*

"*The Book of Adventures 2* is a whirlwind of pleasant insanity. The bizarre characters, and their deadpan wisecracks and strange obsessions, had me laughing many, many times. Gregory Bouthiette strikes again!"
> —Zachary T. Owen, author of *Burn Down the House and Everyone In It*

"This book could easily be a video game. It should be. I can play along in my mind. Books like this are a special kind of magic. I love it."
> —S.T. Cartledge, author of *Kaiju Canyon*

CB555-06: The Book of Adventures 2
ISBN: 978-0-9962768-9-4

Carrion Blue 555
Chicopee MA / Lambertville NJ
carrionblue555@gmail.com

Cover art copyright ©2016 by Matthew Revert.
www.matthewrevert.com
Carrion Blue 555 logo designed by Brent Carpentier.

"This is Heaven alright, but there's a man outside with a gun."
—Cardiacs, "What Paradise is Like"

TABLE OF CONTENTS

Thanks to Joejoe and Josh for continuing to help me make my books as great as possible.

Thanks to Matt for making the best covers ever.

Thanks to Zach, Shane, and Max for writing awesome blurbs for my book.

This book is dedicated to my family, my friends, and anyone who supports my work.

THE ADVENTURES OF JAKE AND MASON

MASON

Hey, uh, Jake? I know that our big blue friend told us
that we can be here, and that should be enough time to
make our three wishes, but maybe we should just take
The Wishing Flower back with us...

ALEX

Just keep on looking for those special Powers. Those
Powers are really awesome to have, but we cannot get
them unless one of us finds them. You know what to
do.

RYAN

Deal with any people that come here from the City. We
will attack them if they dare to come here.

MASON

I know that we are here to make some wishes, Jake, but
this place still scares me a little... Whoa! Ouch... Huh?
Oh man, this dumb bomb is getting in the way. Now
look at that little yellow flower, Jake! It's so beautiful...
The old Masters keep on talking about the people that
made this place. I just don't know why. Maybe they just
like telling us the same story whenever they come to
visit us at Sammy's house. Whoa! How did you do that?
Jake, I think we're in trouble! You deal with him, I'm
gonna be making my wishes first... I wish I was seven
years old again... And I wish I had a backpack with
me... And I also wish that I had a lot of underwear in
my backpack. Just in case... Okay, Jake, I made my
three wishes. I know that it was a little long, but they
were the three things I've always wanted... What's
wrong, buddy? Oh yeah! Right! The plant, I forgot
about it... Wait, hold on. I just need to check to see if
I'm already wearing little kid underwear: yes, I am.
And they don't have any cartoon stuffs on them, which
is the only underwear I like to wear: with no cartoon
stuffs on them. Now let's get the plant and head back to

the City, buddy.

RYAN
Aha! There are the Powers...

***

SAMMY

Oh, hey guys. How was making your three wishes from
The Wishing Flower?

MASON

It was fun, Sammy, but I was the only one that made
my three wishes. Jake didn't have a chance to do it.

SAMMY

It's okay, I'm sure that Jake will make his wishes when
he's ready, Mason. I'm just glad to see you got your
three wishes done.

MASON

Yeah, I hope that he will make his wishes soon, but he
still can't talk, Sammy. What are we gonna do with
him?

SAMMY

Don't worry, Mason. I'm sure that Jake will talk
someday, buddy. But in the meantime, I have
something to tell you guys: I heard that there is some
bad stuff going on in our City—I need you guys to go
through the portal to get some training on the way, so
that you guys will be ready to pay a visit to my old
friend Bryan... But the only way to get to his place is
through the lava. I'm sure that you guys can do it
together, but you guys can't just walk through it...

EMMA

But you could fly over it! I was just coming up here to
tell you guys that I was working on a little something to
help you get to Bryan's place, but I just need some help
building the thing. Right, Dad?

SAMMY

Yes, Emma, that might work. But why would you want
these boys to help you out, anyway?

EMMA

It's just to see how good they are, for when they become heroes someday. And I know that these guys will do a good job on building the ride to get to your friend Bryan's place, Dad. And I also know that we have nice little heroes here.

MASON

Well, we are not heroes yet, Emma, but I can try and help you out to build that ride for me and Jake here.

SAMMY

Whoa, slow down there, Mason. You guys will never last a second without training. Before you do anything else, you better go through my portal and get some training on a nice little island.

MASON

Okay, Sammy. We will get started on our training on the little island now, but do we need to bring The Wishing Flower with us? I'd hate to have it on me while we are training.

SAMMY

Get in there before I make my own wish and turn you both into giant spiders.

***

EMMA
Just get your training out of the way, then come back to
the City through the portal... This is a fake big monster:
it may look scary, but it's not very hard to free yourself
from it. Put Mason in that thing and try to free him,
Jake. This is good practice in case one of you gets eaten
by any monsters in the City. Go ahead and try it, Jake.

MASON
Okay, Jake, just go with me inside the fake monster's
tummy. I don't like being eaten by any monsters,
buddy... Whoa, uh, thanks, Jake. I really liked it that
you saved me from that fake monster.

SAMMY
That's the big door that you need to go through, but it's
kind of locked. There should be a key somewhere to
open it, just look around for it.

MASON
Hey, Jake, I found the key. Let's open the door now.

SAMMY
Those are some bad creatures down there, you do not
want to mess around with them. If you guys can take
down five of them, the rest should go away... Good
training, boys. I'm confident you guys are ready to
head out and do some hero stuff now.

MASON
Yeah, but we don't want to delay helping out the people
in the City, Sammy. We got the moves, right, Jake?
We'd like to stay and chat, Sammy, but we need to get a
move on with our adventure.

SAMMY
Okay, fine. You guys can go out and go on your
adventure. And while you guys are out, I may need you

two to help me out with a little something.

MASON
What do you need, Sammy?

SAMMY
I may need you to go visit a friend of mine at the store
where he works. You'll need to let him know I have
some things to give to two good friends of mine.

MASON
You got it, Sammy. We'll do that for you. Right, Jake?

SAMMY
Okay, thanks, guys. I really owe you one.

***

MASON
Hey, Emma, what is this thing that you're working on
here?

EMMA
I'm glad that you asked, Mason: this is the ride that I
was telling you guys about.

MASON
Wow, it looks so cool! Do you want us to do anything
for you?

EMMA
I don't need you guys to help me out yet. I will let you
know if I need any help.

MASON
Okay, Emma. Just let us know if you need any help on
your sweet ride.

EMMA
Okay, Mason, I will let you guys know if I need any
help finishing this thing.

MASON
Hey, Jake, look! I think that guy needs some help to
bring bad guys down. Let's go ask him, buddy... Hey,
excuse me, sir, do you need any help taking these guys
down?

MIKE
Yes, I do, kid... You actually want to help me out?

MASON
Yes, we would like to help you out, uh, what's your
name, sir?

MIKE
My name is Mike. And what are your names?

MASON
My name is Mason, and this is my friend Jake. We are
hoping to become heroes someday.

MIKE
Well, if you guys can take ten of these guards down, I'll
give you guys some 10-Coins.

MASON
Okay, Mike, we will take them down right now. Let's do
this, Jake... Yeah, we did it, Jake! Let's go talk to Mike
again... Hey, Mike, we took down all ten guards for
you.

MIKE
Well, thank you for the help, guys! Here's the 10-Coins
that I promised, here you go.

MASON
Okay, thanks, Mike.

MIKE
Any time, boys. And thanks again for the help.

MASON
Hey, Jake, do you think we should go see if Emma
needs help now? Yeah, I'm thinking the same thing,
too, buddy. Let's go... Hello again, Emma. Do you need
our help now?

EMMA
Yes, I do need your help now, guys.

MASON
Okay, and what do you want us to do, Emma?

EMMA
I just need you guys to make a path for me to bring this up to the lava. After you do that, I need you guys to go get some more 10-Coins from someone else that needs help; maybe you guys can go ask my dad if he needs you.

MASON
Okay, Emma, you can count on us! Right, Jake? Yeah, that's right, my friend.

EMMA
Okay, thanks, guys. I know that I can count on the both of you.

MASON
Hey, if you need any help from us, Emma, you can always ask us any time.

EMMA
Okay, Mason, how about less talking and more pushing, buddy.

MASON
Oh, okay. Sorry, Emma. I'll shut up now.

EMMA
Thank you... Alright, guys, that's good! Thanks for the help.

MASON
Any time, Emma. We always like to help you out. And your father, too.

EMMA
Yeah, I know, Mason. Now how about you guys go and see if more people need any help?

MASON
Okay, Emma, we will. And you're welcome... Hello
there, do you need help with anything?

OWEN
Well, I might need some help with my power... You see,
I need some help with that thing on my roof because I
don't have any power for my house.

MASON
So what do you need us to do?

OWEN
Well I might need you guys to go out to the power
station and see what is happening. I'll give you 10-
Coins if you do.

MASON
No problem. We'll go see what's going on, and then we
will get your power back for you.

OWEN
Okay, thanks. I know that I can count you guys.

MASON
There's the power station, Jake. Let's go turn his power
back on... Hey, Jake, I bet you could throw me up to
that switch. I'll hop in my underwear first, then you can
throw me up. Let's do it, buddy! Yes! The power is back
on, Jake! Now let's go back and talk to Owen.

OWEN
Hey, you guys got my power back! Thanks for the help.
Now here's your 10-Coins that I promised.

MASON
Cool! Thanks, Owen. Come on, Jake, let's go and see if
Sammy needs any help now... Hey, Sammy, do you

need any help?

SAMMY
Umm, well, I think I might need you guys to go back to
that island you guys got The Wishing Flower from and
fight off some guards there.

MASON
No problem, Sammy. We can do that for you.

SAMMY
Okay, thanks, guys. When you guys get back from the
island, I got something else for you to do.

MASON
Okay, Sammy. We'll try and make it back in time.

SAMMY
Okay, thanks, guys. I'll be waiting for you guys here
when you come back.

MASON
Oh great, we're back on this island again! No matter.
We just have to deal with some guards for Sammy, and
then we can get back and see what kind of other stuff
he has for us, Jake. Sorry, I should just shut up. Let's
just get a move now... Jake, look! It's the guards that
we need to deal with. Let's go take them down, buddy...
That's all the guards, Jake. Now let's go back to the City
and see what Sammy want us to do next... Hey,
Sammy, we're back! What do we need to do now?

SAMMY
Well, I'm glad you asked, Mason: I need you guys to
unclog my big air conditioning machines on the other
side of the City. You guys will need to find your own
way there.

MASON
You can count on us, Sammy. We'll unclog your
machines for you in no time.

SAMMY
That's what I like to hear, Mason.

MASON
There are the machines, Jake! We just have to unclog
them for Sammy. But how do we unclog them?

SAMMY
[walkie talkie]
I think I have an idea for you guys. Mason, if you can
hop in Jake's underwear again, you can destroy the
rocks that are clogging my machines.

MASON
Oh. Okay, Sammy, I can do that. What do you think,
Jake? Are you up for it, buddy? Yeah, Jake is up for it.

SAMMY
Good. Now hop in your underwear, buddy. I'll talk to
you guys later.

MASON
Okay, Jake, that's all the machines! Now let's go see
Emma.

EMMA
You guys are back! Do you have all the 10-Coins?

MASON
Yes, we do, Emma. What do we do now?

EMMA
You guys have to hop on my vehicle, get to the other
side of the lava, and open the portal for me and my

dad. After you do that, we'll know what to do next.

MASON
Okay, Emma. You can count on us.

EMMA
Good luck, guys.

***

MASON
There's the end, Jake!

SAMMY
Whoa! Man, I cannot get over how far we can go in these things.

EMMA
Oh no, we got some bad news, dad.

SAMMY
What's the bad news, Emma?

EMMA
There's a big huge Monster destroying the City! It's really bad!

MASON
Oh great. What now, Sammy? Do we have to go out there and fight that Monster? Please say no, please say no...

SAMMY HERMIT
I'm sorry, Mason, but you guys will have to do it. You guys might need to get more 10-Coins first, though. Good luck.

MASON
Hey, Jake, I see someone that needs some help... Umm, excuse me? Yeah, uh, do you need any help?

BUBBLE BOB
Why yes, I do need some help. I can get this air conditioning machine working, but I'll need some 10-Coins.

MASON
That sounds like a job for us. Right, Jake?

BUBBLE BOB
Okay, I'll let you guys do it for me. Get as many 10-Coins as you can, and I'll let you keep any I don't need.

MASON
Okay, Bubble Bob. We'll be back soon... Hey, Jake, look! I can see something over there... It looks like a race! Should we be in the race, Jake? Hey, fellows, is it okay if me and my friend here join in?

AL
Uh, sure. If you guys win, I will give you ten 10-Coins. Not that you'll ever win.

MASON
Okay, let's do this.

AL
First to cross the finish line after three laps wins! Uh... Whoa, I never thought I'd say this, but you guys proved me wrong! Here's the ten 10-Coins I promised you.

MASON
Wow, thanks, Al! We're very happy about this.

AL
Thanks for racing.

MASON
Hey, it's what heroes do... Hey, Jake, look! There's a guy that needs help with something over there... Uh, hello there! Umm, do you need any help here, sir?

LARRY 2x4
Yes, I do, little one. I need some help making more pathways to that big Monster up there.

MASON
Okay, is there anything that we can do to help?

LARRY 2x4
I may need you guys to bring me some 10-Coins so I can build the pathway for any heroes that are brave enough to stop that Monster.

MASON
Well, you have two brave heroes right in front of you. I think we can get some more 10-Coins for you, sir.

LARRY 2x4
Oh good. Thank you, little one. When you guys come back with the 10-Coins, I can build that pathway.

MASON
Thanks, Larry. We'll be back soon... Hey, umm, excuse me, Bubble Bob. We are back with those 10-Coins we promised you.

BUBBLE BOB
Thanks, guys. Here are the 10-Coins that I don't need.

MASON
Oh good. Thanks, Bubble Bob. Let's go find Larry 2x4 again, Jake... Larry... Larry! We got the 10-Coins that you asked for.

LARRY 2x4
Thanks again, little one.

MASON
Can you build that pathway for us now, please?

LARRY 2x4
Sure, little one. I can build that pathway for you guys now.

MASON

Hey, Sammy, Emma: we got enough 10-Coins for the weapon. Can we fire it up now?

SAMMY

Yeah, sure, we can finally fire this weapon up. Stand back, guys, this might get a little rough.

EMMA

Come here, Mason, I can hold you buddy.

MASON

Umm, Emma, I'm a big kid now. I don't need you to hold me anymore.

EMMA

Umm, Mason, you are seven years old again. Besides, you used to like me holding you a lot.

MASON

Okay, fine. You can hold me just this one time.

SAMMY

Okay, guys, you can go up there now and destroy that big bad Monster. And don't forget to turn on the next portal when you guys get to my other friend's house.

MASON

Don't worry, Sammy, we can do this as a team. You can count on us.

SAMMY

I know, Mason. I'm just a little worried.

EMMA

It's okay, Dad. Jake and Mason can do this like the little heroes they are.

MASON
Yeah, Sammy, we can do this like the little heroes we are. Now let's go, Jake... Whoa, that is one huge Monster! Those people in the City weren't kidding around. Let's do this, Jake... Whoa! Ahhhhh! Jake, help! This Monster just ate me! I need you to fight this Monster now, and fast.

SAMMY
Jake, you have to save Mason from that big Monster. You know what to do. Now go save him.

MASON
That's it, Jake, keep on fighting the Monster so I can get out this gross stomach of his... Whoa! Ahhhhh! Ahhhhh! Ow... Thanks, Jake. That was not fun at all.

EMMA
Good work saving Mason, Jake. Now you guys need to get a move on, my dad and I are waiting for you.

MASON
Don't worry, Emma, you can count on us. Let's go, Jake.

***

SAMMY

Whoa, ouch! Man, my friend sure likes to make a mess
of his own home. And his home was dirty to begin with.

ALEX

Well well well, look who we have here, Ryan. It seems
that our old friend Sammy has finally come to join the
dark side.

RYAN

Yeah, you're right, Alex: our old friend Sammy, who's
looked the same since he was six years old.

SAMMY

Wait, Alex? Ryan? What are you guys doing here? I had
hoped you guys were still on my side. And what have
you guys done to Bryan?

ALEX

Oh, Sammy, you just don't get it, do you? You see, after
you left LA, we decided to become evil. So we're evil
now. And here you are, still prancing with the good
guys, when you had a chance to become one of us.

RYAN

But no, you wanted to stay as a good guy! Like those
dumb little heroes with you. Why did you turn your
back on us, Sammy?

SAMMY

Because you guys were acting evil! You know I don't
like evil people. I thought you were still good guys, but
I guess I was wrong. You're evil now.

ALEX

And we're happy to be evil, Sammy! And we're sorry,
Sammy, but we have to go now.

RYAN
Oh, and Sammy, say goodbye to your Bryan—you won't
be seeing him again.

ALEX
And say goodbye to your little friend Mason ever being
seventeen again, because he's going to be a seven year-
old kid forever.

MASON
Wait, what? Sammy, what were they talking about?

SAMMY
I'm sorry, Mason, but wishes to The Wishing Flower
are forever. You wished to be seven years old again,
and now you will be. Forever. Maybe we can somehow
use The Wishing Flower to change you back...

MASON
Oh. I didn't know that, Sammy. I'm sorry, I'll do my
wish again.

EMMA
No, Mason, you can't do your wish again. We can't lose
you like that again.

MASON
Thanks, Emma. I'm glad that you really like me as a
seven year-old again. That's why you asked if you can
hold me.

EMMA
Yes, I did, Mason. And Jake really likes it when you are
a seven year-old boy, too. That was when you guys met
for the first time.

SAMMY
Sorry to interrupt, Emma, but I need Jake and Mason

to go find some more 10-Coins for us now. We can continue talking about this later.

MASON
You got it, Sammy. Come on, Jake, let's go find some more 10-Coins, buddy... Hey, Jake, look! There's people in this cave. Let's go see if they need any help... Umm, hello there! Uh, do you guys need any help?

MATT
Yes, we do, little one. You see, me and my friend Brandon are trying to get this diamond out of the wall here, and we tried everything to get it out but nothing's working.

BRANDON
If you guys can help us get this diamond out of the wall, we will happily give you guys some 10-Coins.

MASON
You can count on us! Let's go Jake... Whoa, this place is really amazing on the inside. I never got to see anything this awesome back in Miami, Jake... Okay, enough talking. Let's just get this diamond... Okay, Matt and Brandon, we got the diamond out of the wall!

MATT
Okay, good. Thanks, little one. And here's the 10-Coins we promised you guys.

BRANDON
And here's the 10-Coins that I have for you guys as well.

MASON
Wow, thanks, guys! Come on, Jake, let's go see if Emma is ready... Hey, Emma, are you ready for us now?

EMMA
Umm, not yet, Mason. But I think I saw a spider cave.
Maybe you guys can find some 10-Coins in there.

MASON
Umm, Emma, you know that I'm afraid of spiders,
right?

EMMA
Oh yeah, right. Sorry, Mason, I just forgot about that.
Maybe Jake can go in there by himself while you wait
outside.

MASON
Okay, that's a good idea. Thanks, Emma.

EMMA
No problem Mason, I'll be waiting for you guys when
you come back.

MASON
Whoa, this is a scary spider cave, Jake. I'll wait right
here on this rock until you come out, buddy... Jake,
you're back! You got more 10-Coins, awesome! Now
let's go see Emma again, buddy... Hey, Emma! We got
more 10-Coins. Are we ready to go through this hot
place now?

EMMA
Yes, you are ready now, Mason. Be careful: when you
guys go through here, there might be some guards
trying to stop you. Don't forget to run them over if you
can.

MASON
You got it, Emma. We can do this...

***

MASON
There's some guards there, Jake, run them over! Hey, Emma, where's Sammy?

EMMA
Jake, Mason! My dad has been kidnapped by Alex and Ryan! They took him to their hideout, and I need you guys to go there and save him, please.

MASON
Don't worry, Emma, we will save your dad for you. You just stay here and wait for us to open the elevator for you.

EMMA
Thanks, Mason. I will be waiting at the elevator.

SAMMY
Jake, Mason, it's good to see you guys. Thanks for coming to save me.

MASON
No problem, Sammy, but how are we going to get you out of that cage?

SAMMY
I think the only way out of this cage is using a switch. Be sure to free my friend Bryan, too. He's over there.

MASON
Don't worry, Sammy, you can count on us. Come on, Jake, let's go free Bryan and Sammy, buddy... Psst, Bryan! Bryan, down here.

BRYAN
Oh, hello, guys! Sammy has told me all about you, and I want to say thanks for coming to free us.

MASON
You're welcome, Bryan. Is there a switch somewhere to get you free from that cage?

BRYAN
Yes, there is a switch right up there. But it might be challenging to get up there.

MASON
Hmm, maybe we can try that door over there. Might be a way up to that switch... Come on, Jake, let's go! We'll be back, Bryan, just stay there.

BRYAN
Like I have a choice.

MASON
Okay, Bryan, you're free now.

BRYAN
Thank you, guys. I have always trusted your friend Sammy. For a long time, ever since we were kids...

SAMMY
Hey, uh, guys... I still need some help over here, please.

BRYAN
You guys follow me. I know where the other switch is to free Sammy.

MASON
Come on, Jake. Bryan is gonna show us where the last switch is, buddy.

BRYAN
Here it is, guys: just pull it, and you can free your friend Sammy.

SAMMY
Thank you, Bryan. And you too, Jake and Mason. It's a
good thing that I kept The Wishing Flower in my
pocket. It didn't get crushed.

ALEX
Thank you for giving us The Wishing Flower, Sammy.
Now we can go on to the next stage of our plan, Ryan.

MASON
No! We need to get The Wishing Flower back! Sammy,
what are we going to do now?

SAMMY
I think you guys need to go up there and stop Alex and
Ryan, once and for all.

MASON
But how are we gonna get up there, Sammy?

BRYAN
I can throw you guys there.

MASON
Okay! Thanks, Bryan. We owe you one.

BRYAN
Any time, guys. Now hold on, and... Jump!

MASON
Sammy, open the elevator for Emma!

SAMMY
You got it, Mason. I can do that for you guys.

EMMA
Hey, Dad, Bryan! Do you guys need some help to get to
the roof?

SAMMY
Thanks, Emma. Now let's get a move on.

BRYAN
We need to watch Jake and Mason stop Alex and Ryan,
you guys.

EMMA
I'm on it, Bryan.

MASON
Whoa, that's one huge robot that they have there! And
there's Alex and Ryan, Jake! And they've got The
Wishing Flower with them! Are you ready for this,
Jake? Good, me too.

ALEX
Now that we have The Wishing Flower, Ryan, no one in
this City will be able to stop us.

RYAN
You can say that again, Alex. Can you believe Sammy
and Bryan are still trying to be heroes while we're being
evil villains? We can take over this whole world.

ALEX
Yeah, I have to agree with you, Ryan.

MASON
Stop right there, Alex and Ryan. I think you guys are
forgetting two more heroes here.

ALEX
No! How can you guys be here?

MASON
Our new friend Bryan threw us up here.

RYAN
Well, you guys are too late now! We already have The
Wishing Flower, and you guys will need to fight us to
get it back.

MASON
Uh, yeah. Ryan: it's our plan to do that, because you
guys are evil, and we are good.

ALEX
Enough talking, Mason.

MASON
Let's do this, Jake!

EMMA
There they are!

SAMMY
Oh no! Alex and Ryan got a huge robot, and they can
use it to fight them.

BRYAN
Don't worry Sammy, those boys are heroes now. Like
us. We just need to stay up here and watch your boys
become true heroes. Like us.

SAMMY
Okay, Bryan.

ALEX
No! This isn't happening! We cannot lose like this!

RYAN
And our robot can't take another hit like that, Alex.

MASON
Come on, Jake, we need to finish that robot.

RYAN
No, not like this! Not like this!

MASON
Yes! We did it, Jake! Alex and Ryan are done for, and
they are melting in that lava now, and... Oh no! So is
The Wishing Flower!

SAMMY
Yes! You guys did it! Alex and Ryan are done now.

EMMA
But Mason, now we can't change you back...

MASON
It's okay, Emma. I finally accepted that I like being
seven years old forever.

SAMMY
Whatever makes you happy, Mason. You made that
wish yourself, buddy.

MASON
Hey, Bryan, what's wrong?

BRYAN
We might not be happy anytime soon, you guys.

SAMMY
What do you mean, Bryan?

BRYAN
I mean, what if Alex and Ryan did not really get done
in by that lava?

SAMMY
Come on, Bryan, those guys will never come back. Once
you are melted from lava, you are really gone for good.

BRYAN
Yeah, you're right, Sammy. Let's go back to your place
and have some fun now.

SAMMY
Hey, Emma, are you going to give Jake and Mason
kisses now?

EMMA
Yes, I am, Dad. I'll do it right now... Come here, Jake, I
got you a little something, buddy...

MASON
Hey, Emma, do you have one for me, too?

EMMA
Yes, I do, Mason... There you go, buddy.

MASON
Thanks, Emma. I'll keep it on my face forever.

SAMMY
Hey, you guys, come over here! Look what I found.

MASON
What is it, Sammy?

SAMMY
It looks like a huge portal. Come, Bryan. Help me bring
it back to my place.

BRYAN
You got it, Sammy.

EMMA
Whoa, that's one huge portal.

MASON
Hey, Emma. Do you wanna race back to Sammy's
house?

EMMA
Sure, Mason. I'll race you back to my dad's house.

MASON
Oh, I'm going to beat you there, Emma!

EMMA
That's what you think, Mason.

THE ADVENTURES OF JAKE AND MASON

2

SAMMY

Hey! Jake, Mason, Emma, wake up, you guys! Today is
the day.

MASON

Uh, Sammy, we're already outside.

SAMMY

Oh, okay. I'm on my way right now, guys.

EMMA

Take your time, Dad. We'll wait out here.

MASON

And don't forget, Emma, I need to find out what this
big portal can do again.

SAMMY

Mason, please don't touch anything. I don't think you'll
be able to figure out what it does, buddy.

EMMA

Well, you may not know yet, Dad, but that doesn't
mean Mason can't try.

SAMMY

We just need to wait for my old friend Bryan. I invited
him to come along with us through this big portal.

BRYAN

Hey! Hi, guys, sorry that I'm late. Are we ready to go
through this thing now, Sammy?

SAMMY

Yes, we are, Bryan. Now let's see if we can figure out
what this portal can really do. Mason, would like to
give it a go?

MASON
Why, yes I would, Sammy. I would like to figure it out.

EMMA
Sorry, Mason, but it looks like Jake just beat you to it!

MASON
Whoa, it looks like this thing here is some kind of key
that activates the portal.

BRYAN
Whoa! Look at that, you guys.

WILLIAM
Finally, the last portal has been opened!

MASON
Ah! What are those things!

SAMMY
I'm not sure, Mason, but I think we'll find out soon...

WILLIAM
Yes! You cannot hide from me now, you little punks.

EMMA
Do something, Jake!

MASON
What does this do? Or that? How about this? Press all
the buttons!

WILLIAM
Come to me now, you fools.

EMMA
Who was that guy?

SAMMY
Hang on, you guys. This could get a little crazy.

BRYAN
I'm already hanging on, Sammy! You don't have to tell
me twice!

MASON
Jake, I want off this thing!

EMMA
Ahhhhhhhhhh!

SAMMY
Stay safe, Jake and Mason...

***

MASON
Okay, I swear, that's the last time that I ever, ever,
touch anything, Jake.

GUARD 999
There he is! Move in. Step away from the boy.

DRYAN
No, no, he might want to watch this. We'll take the boy
with us. Now let's go.

MASON
Umm, excuse me, sir. Where are you taking us?

DRYAN
It's okay, kid. You guys are going to be fine. We just
want to do a little test on your friend there.

MASON
Wait, what? What are you talking about?

DRYAN
I mean, that I want you to watch what we do to your
friend.

MASON
Who, Jake?

DRYAN
Yes.

MASON
Umm. Okay, I'll go, too.

BARON HAX
That's enough, Dryan.

DRYAN
Sorry, Baron.

BARON HAX
I think this one is going to be a big help to fight against
the Metal Creatures.

DRYAN
Sorry to interrupt, Hax, but I think the Metal Creatures
are on their way to the City right now. We need some
help to stop them.

BARON HAX
I don't intend to lose this war against those things.
Move forward with the plan. And finish up with our
new friend here tonight.

DRYAN
As you wish, Hax. I'll be back later, Jake. Mason, you
can come get your buddy now.

MASON
Okay. Thanks, Dryan. Hey, Jake, did they put those
new Powers in you?

JAKE
Yes, they did, Mason. And I've got some good news,
buddy: I can talk now.

MASON
That's cool, Jake. Come on, we need to get out of here,

JAKE
Wait for me, Mason! I need to put my shoes on.

MASON
Hey, Jake, do you remember how to jump?

JAKE
Yes, I do remember how to jump, Mason. Why?

MASON
I was just asking.

JAKE
Oh.

MASON
And do you remember how to roll, Jake?

JAKE
Yes, I do remember how to roll. Just watch this.

MASON
Uh, Jake… I think we may need to jump up to that
ledge there… I'm not so sure about this.

JAKE
It's okay, Mason, I'll help you. Just hop on my back,
and I'll jump up there.

MASON
Okay, Jake, I will… Jake, there's a guard blocking us!
Can you fight him, please?

JAKE
Just stand back, Mason, this might be a little tough.

GUARD 214
Surrender!

MASON
Nice one, Jake. He hit the ground pretty hard.

JAKE
Hey, thanks. I've been learning new moves from

Sammy... I hope we find him, and Emma, too.

MASON
And don't forget Bryan, Jake. We can't forget about
Bryan.

JAKE
Yeah, sorry, Mason. I did forget about Bryan.

MASON
Well, you know what they say...

JAKE
Yes, I do know what they say, Mason. Now stop talking
so we can get a move on.

MASON
I know. You got it, Jake.

GUARD 196
There he is! Get him!

GUARD 7878
Prisoners on Level 2.

GUARD 196
I think I've got them...

MASON
I think you can slam down on the floor here, Jake. It's
time to break stuff.

JAKE
You said it, Mason. Breaking stuff is fun.

MASON
Jake, quiet.

JAKE
Why?

MASON
There are two guards there. Let's listen to them...

JAKE
Okay.

GUARD 2319
Have you been to the City races this week?

GUARD 590
I'll be there, dude.

GUARD 2319
I've been on duty for two days!

GUARD 590
Hey, don't complain. I have sewer duty next week.

GUARD 2319
Oh, you poor boob. Which commander did you tick off
this time?

GUARD 590
I don't think Dryan is going to win the race next week,
dude.

GUARD 2319
You're just asking to get shot by saying that.

GUARD 590
Sorry.

MASON
Okay, Jake, let's take them down.

JAKE
Yeah, I've had enough of their talking.

GUARD 590
You're busted.

MASON
Hey, Jake, I can see the door! Let's go.

JAKE
Wait for me, Mason. I don't want to lose you, buddy.

MASON
We're free, Jake! Thanks to me, of course. It's nice to get some fresh air again. We'll help that Baron Hax guy, alright.

JAKE
Yeah, I was just thinking the same thing, Mason. Let's get a move on.

***

CARCOSA CADEN
Hello, strangers. My name is Caden. Can I help you guys out with anything?

JAKE
Uh, yes. We need to find out more about these Metal Creatures. Do you know anything about them, Caden?

CARCOSA CADEN
Umm, no. Sorry, friend, I don't really know anything about the Metal Creatures. But I think I may know someone who knows everything about the Metal Creatures...

MASON
Do you think that you can show us where they are?

CARCOSA CADEN
Oh, I'm afraid I can't do that. I need to take care of this little boy here. But perhaps you guy wouldn't mind helping us out. Looks like some guards are on their way...

GUARD 64
We are sorry to interrupt, but we can't let you get away from us. Surrender and die!

MASON
Umm, excuse me, sir. Do you mean surrender or die?

CARCOSA CADEN
We need you guys to help us out. Clear these guards away for us, and I will help as I can.

GUARD 590
Stop there!

GUARD 7878
Shoot them! Shoot them!

GUARD 64
You're busted.

GUARD 1777
Calling all guards! Calling all guards!

GUARD 7878
Say goodbye!

MASON
Whoa! That was fun... Right, Jake?

JAKE
Yeah, it was fun, Mason. I think I've gotten used to
these new Powers now.

CARCOSA CADEN
That was cool, my new friends.

MASON
Thanks, Caden. We're kind of new to this, not really
heroes yet.

CARCOSA CADEN
But I think you guys are heroes now. Thank you again
for saving us. Now I need to get this boy back to my
place. He must observe me.

MASON
This kid, he looks a little scared to me.

GUARD 2319
Move along.

CARCOSA CADEN
I thank you again, but I really need to go now. I believe
we will see each other again soon.

MASON
Hey, wait, Caden! What about us?

CARCOSA CADEN
Oh, I'm sorry. If you're looking for someone to help
against the Metal Creatures, ask for Zorn. He can help
you.

JAKE
Okay, thanks, Caden.

MASON
Come on, Jake, let's go find this guy named Zorn.

JAKE
You got it. Let's go find him, Mason.

***

JAKE
We're looking for a guy named Zorn. Caden sent us.
Umm... Are you Zorn?

MASON
It is him, Jake, but I don't think he's happy to see us.

ZORN
New faces make me a little mad. Maybe I will let you
guys join me, but I need you to do something for me
first.

JAKE
How can we help?

ZORN
I need you guys to go and steal Baron Hax's flag from
the junkyard and bring it back to me. Then maybe we'll
talk.

MASON
We can do that for you, Zorn. You can count on us.
Let's get a move on, Jake.

JAKE
I'm sorry about him, Zorn, he's not really a normal kid.
Come on, buddy, let's get out of here.

MASON
Whoa, look at this place, Jake! I have never seen
anything as cool as this before.

JAKE
Come on, Mason, we need to steal the flag for Zorn.

MASON
Oh right, sorry. Wait for me!

MASON
There it is, Jake. Would you like to get it?

JAKE
I was thinking about it. Just stay behind me, I don't
know what's gonna happen.

MASON
Whoa! Ahhhhhhh! Ow!

ZORN
[walkie talkie]
Yeah, I think you guys are in the gang now.

MASON
Jake, can we go back to the City now?

JAKE
Yeah, let's head back to the City, Mason.

MASON
I need you to carry me, please.

JAKE
Sure thing, buddy. I don't mind.

MASON
You know, Jake, I kind of miss Emma doing this for
me.

JAKE
I know. We'll try to find her soon.

***

MASON
Whoa, being a little hero sure makes you thirsty.

ZORN
I wouldn't drink that water.

MASON
What happened to the water?

ZORN
Baron Hax turned off the water in the City, trying to
redirect it and drown the Metal Creatures. But he
messed up. I disagreed with it when I was a guard.
That's why I quit.

MASON
You used to be a guard for Baron Hax? Maybe he
thought you were a little hard to work with...

ZORN
I quit on my own terms, Mason. Anyways, I think I
found a way to turn the water back on.

MASON
You did?

ZORN
I did.

JAKE
How are we going to turn the water back on, Zorn?

ZORN
The only way to turn on the water back on is to go
outside the City and turn on the valves at the water
station.

JAKE
Outside the City? But what about the security wall?

MASON
And what about the Metal Creatures! I just know
they're going to be waiting for us out there. And you
haven't told us anything about them yet, Zorn.

ZORN
Don't worry, I will tell you guys everything about the
Metal Creatures soon. But first, the water station.

MASON
You can count on us.

JAKE
Mason, hop on.

MASON
What is this thing, Jake?

JAKE
It's a car, buddy. Just hang on to me, we're about to go
fast.

MASON
Okay, Jake. I will.

GUARD 7878
I hate the smell from this part of the City.

JAKE
Here it is, Mason. That's the door to the water station.

MASON
I don't know about this, Jake... I think I'll stay in the
car, if you don't mind.

JAKE
Sorry, Mason, but you have to come with me. It's just
the two of us now. I don't want to lose you, too.

MASON
Okay, Jake, I'll go with you. But I'm not going to like it.

JAKE
You'll just have to deal with it, buddy.

MASON
Jake, those are the Metal Creatures!

JAKE
Whoa! These Creatures aren't friendly at all, Mason.

MASON
You think I don't know that!

JAKE
No, sorry. What kind of Metal Creatures are they,
anyway?

MASON
I think there are scorpions, and bugs, and other kinds,
too.

JAKE
Alright... Hey, wait. Mason, how do we defeat these
Metal Creatures?

MASON
The only way to defeat them is by punching them,
buddy. Unless you have a cool toy with you.

JAKE
And how do you actually know about this?

MASON
This guy Dryan told me when I was with him.

JAKE
Mason, how many times did Sammy tell you to not go
out on your own?

MASON
Seven. He told me seven times.

JAKE
Yeah. So if he asks you to go with him again, tell me
first.

MASON
Okay, Jake. I will.

JAKE
Thank you.

MASON
Where is this valve anyway? This place is really big.

JAKE
Just keep on looking, Mason. I'm sure it's around here
somewhere.

MASON
We just have to stick together and find it as a team.
What do you think?

JAKE
I think that's a good idea, Mason. Now let's get a move
on.

MASON
Man, these Metal Creatures just keep getting in the
way!

JAKE
You're right, but these punks are almost gone now.

MASON
Good, because I've had enough of these guys.

JAKE
Look, I can see the valve from here.

MASON
Oh, good! Let's go... And here we are! Let me handle
this, Jake... Uh. I think I might need you to help me,
please.

JAKE
Let me at it... There you go, Mason.

MASON
Thanks, you're a really big help.

JAKE
Thanks, Mason, that means a lot to me.

MASON
Let's head back to the City now, Jake.

JAKE
Right behind you, Mason.

MASON
Hey look, Jake! The car is still here.

JAKE
Yep, the car is still here waiting for us. Let's head back
to Zorn.

MASON
...And here we are!

ZORN
The water is back on. I'd love to see how Baron Hax is
going to thank us.

JAKE
We've done what you asked. Are you going to tell us
about the Metal Creatures? Can you help us find our
friends? And I want to speak to your leader, too.

ZORN
Just give it time, Jake. I need to make the right plans.
But I have another job for you, while you're waiting.
You know the prison that you guys were at?

MASON
Yeah... What could you possibly want us to do there?

ZORN
I need you guys to head back there and find out what
Baron Hax's guards are up to with the Metal Creatures.
And don't worry: after you guys come back from that,
I'll be happy to give you guys another mission.

MASON
You're sending us to the prison again? What is it with
us having to do everything, and all the stuff all the
time?

JAKE
That's fine. I want Baron Hax to know it's me who's
helping him.

MASON
You know, Jake, I think we should try and make a plan
to blow up the prison.

JAKE
Mason, we can't just blow up the prison, they might be

holding our friends in that place.

MASON
Not the whole place, Jake. I meant we should blow up
just the part that needs to be blown up.

JAKE
Oh, okay. I get it now, Mason. That's a good plan.

MASON
Uh oh, there's a tank in here. We need to be careful
when we go through this place, buddy.

JAKE
Uh, it might be a little too late for that, Mason.

MASON
What do you mean?

JAKE
The tank is chasing us now.

MASON
Ah! What are we waiting for? Move it, Jake!

JAKE
I'm already moving, Mason! Just hold onto me!

GUARD 999
You gonna watch the race?

GUARD 116
Dryan is my boy, he always wins!

GUARD 999
You're busted!

GUARD 116
You are under arrest! Get them!

GUARD 999
Here's some pain...

JAKE
And goodbye, you guys.

MASON
Nice one, Jake, you're really getting the hang of this.

JAKE
Hey, thanks. I learned a lot from Sammy.

MASON
Oh cool, we found a passage to another part of this
City, Jake.

JAKE
Quiet, Mason, let's go see what those guards are up to...

GUARD 590
These Metal Creatures are very helpful when we give
them new Powers.

GUARD 196
And as long as no one sees us, we can keep giving them
Powers!

JAKE
The Metal Creatures are in the City... Why are Baron
Hax's guards giving them Powers?

MASON
I don't know Jake, but we should tell Zorn when we get
back to his place... Uh oh, we're in trouble, Jake.

JAKE
Come on, Mason, we need to get that tank to blow
those others tanks up for us!

MASON
Let's hurry up. I don't like this place, it scares me. Like,
a lot.

JAKE
Don't worry, buddy, we will be fast... Now hurry up,
this place is about to blow!

MASON
Whoa! That was actually kind of fun.

***

MASON
I wish we were back in Miami.

JAKE
Yeah, I don't think we can do that, Mason.

MASON
And why's that, Jake?

JAKE
Because this is Los Angeles, buddy.

MASON
Oh, cool! I've always wanted to live here, Jake, did you
know that?

JAKE
No, I didn't, Mason.

MASON
Ever since I was a little boy, I've always dreamed of
living in Los Angeles. And now that we're in LA, I get to
live my dream!

JAKE
Well, I'm happy that you get to live your dream.

MASON
Yeah. Let's head back to Zorn.

JAKE
Okay. You lead the way this time, buddy.

MASON
The good guys are back and ready for anything!

JAKE
We found out what the guards are up to: it seems that

they are giving the Metal Creatures some new Powers.

ZORN
Really? Our leader will be quite interested to hear that news.

JAKE
So what now, Zorn?

ZORN
I got this guy I want you to go meet. He might even have a little something special for you.

MASON
You can count on us, Zorn.

ZORN
Now get a move on. He expects you in minutes.

JAKE
Let's go, Mason.

MASON
I'm right behind you, Jake.

ZORN
[walkie talkie]
Oh, and by the way, the guy's name is Trew.

JAKE
Be careful, Mason, you don't really know this guy.

MASON
It's okay, Jake, I got this. Yo, Trew, it's good to meet you. We were sent here by your friend Zorn.

TREW
Let me guess, you're Mason, right?

MASON
Yes, I am Mason.

TREW
And that's your good friend, Jake. I've heard a lot about you guys. And I got a new toy here for you, Jake: it's a sword. Be careful, and don't break it.

JAKE
Don't worry, I'm only going to use it to kill some Metal Creatures today.

TREW
Oh yes, The Metal Creatures. How could I forget about those buttheads? I think you should head to the training place and get some practice with that sword, Jake.

JAKE
Okay, I will get some training right now. Let's go, Mason.

MASON
I'm right behind you, Jake.

TREW
Those are some nice friends that Zorn has. Don't you agree?

KIG
Yes, I do, Trew. They'll prove helpful at the water station, I'm sure.

TREW
Oh, don't worry, Kig. You'll get back to the water station soon enough... Awesome training there, Jake. Have you ever thought about being a hero?

JAKE
I can't say that I have, Trew.

TREW
Well, we need heroes like you guys, and I think you
guys will be a great help to us when we fight those
Metal Creatures.

JAKE
Fight Metal Creatures and get toys? Sounds good to
me.

MASON
Slow down, Jake and Trew, I don't think I want to go
back out to the water station and fight more of those
Metal Creatures.

TREW
Don't worry, Mason, you guys will be using that sword
there to help you fight those dorks out there.

MASON
Good point. Okay, I think we can do it.

TREW
I like the sound of that. Maybe Kig can show you guys
the ropes.

KIG
So you want to become heroes? Well, I think I can help
you out with that. We'll head out to the water station to
fight some Metal Creatures and bring some trophies
back to Trew.

MASON
Uh, Kig, I don't like the sound of that.

KIG
Don't worry, Mason, you guys will be safe with me. I
might even show you guys how to fry some big ol'
Metal Creatures while we're out there.

MASON
Whoa, that's a cool weapon that you got there, Kig.
Where did you get it?

TREW
Don't ask. We'll meet at the water station door. And
you better not leave me on my own.

JAKE
Let's do it, Kig.

KIG
I'll meet you guys there.

MASON
I don't know about this, Jake.

JAKE
You'll be fine, buddy.

MASON
Alright. I trust you, Jake.

JAKE
Here we are.

MASON
Okay, let's try and do this.

KIG
Hello, guys. Ready to hunt a few Metal Creatures? Just
follow close and watch my six. This is going to be fun...
Here we go... Here comes trouble!

JAKE
Hey, Mason, let's head up there.

MASON
Okay, Jake, I'm right behind you.

JAKE
And here comes Kig.

KIG
Get behind me while I toast that tank.

MASON
Ah!

JAKE
It's okay, Mason. You're safe, buddy.

MASON
Thanks. I owe you one.

KIG
This way, boys.

JAKE
Wait for us, Kig.

MASON
Yeah, wait for us!

KIG
There's our first target. Keep the other Creatures back
while I fire this guy away.

MASON
Jake, we got some creatures coming from that side.

JAKE
Yeah, I see them, Mason.

KIG
Say goodbye, you little punk.

MASON
And that Metal Creature is down for the count.

KIG
Good work, you guys. Now let's keep on moving.

MASON
We've got company, Kig.

KIG
I know, Mason. Let's destroy these punks together.

JAKE
Kig, there's another one over there.

KIG
Thanks for the heads up, Jake... There's the other
target. Deal with any creatures that might try and stop
me... This guy's going bye-bye now.

JAKE
Ha, that's cool, Kig. You did a thumbs-up, and then a
thumbs-down.

KIG
Thanks, Jake. I've been waiting to do that... We only
have three more left. Now let's get a move on, you
guys...

***

KIG
Thanks for helping me out with those Metal Creatures.
Now I need you boys to bring the trophies back to Trew
for me. I'll be staying here for a while to deal with those
dead Metal Creatures. You did good, boys.

JAKE
Mason, let's go.

MASON
Okay, I'm coming, Jake.

GUARD 7878
Be advised, I'm on foot.

GUARD 845
Do you really have to say that, you dweeb?

GUARD 7878
Yes, I do. Now stop it and keep looking.

GUARD 845
Sorry about that. I'll keep moving now.

JAKE
We need to be careful, Mason. Those guards might see
us carrying these trophies.

MASON
Okay, Jake, I'll be careful.

JAKE
Okay, Mason, we made it.

MASON
Good, I didn't want to get in a fight with those guards
today.

TREW
Hey, welcome back. Where's Kig?

MASON
Kig wanted to stay at the water station and deal with
the dead Metal Creatures. We brought back the
trophies for him.

TREW
Thank you, boys. I think these trophies will be good on
this shelf.

JAKE
I see that you like to collect trophies, Trew.

TREW
Yeah, I always wanted to collect some trophies, ever
since I was a little boy. Now I'm starting to get my
dream.

MASON
I have a dream, too, Trew.

TREW
Oh, really? What's your dream, Mason?

MASON
My dream is to live in Los Angeles, and now that me
and Jake are here, I get to live that dream.

TREW
Well, that's a good dream that you have there, Mason.

JAKE
Do you have another mission for us, Trew?

TREW
Yes, I do have another mission for you boys: I need you
guys to go down in the sewers and deal with four turret

guns down there.

MASON
And how do we destroy those sewer guns?

TREW
With your sword, of course.

JAKE
We'll go do that right now.

TREW
I knew I could count on you boys.

MASON
Uh, Jake? Is this the door to the sewers?

JAKE
Yep, it is. Let's get going.

MASON
Okay, I'm right behind you.

JAKE
Wow, this place is a little dirty.

MASON
Yeah, I would have to agree. Let's just get this mission
done fast... Ah, we found the first gun, Jake!

JAKE
Don't worry, Mason, just wait here. I'm going in.

TREW
[walkie talkie]
That's one gun down, boys! Just keep going, there are
only three left.

MASON
Uh oh, we got company, Jake.

JAKE
Don't worry, Mason, I'll deal with these nerd dorks.

MASON
I need to find out what a nerd dork is...

JAKE
Okay, Mason, the Metal Creatures are gone.

MASON
Good. Thanks, Jake. I think those things are kind of
scary.

JAKE
It's okay, Mason, you're safe with me. I won't let
anything happen to you, I promise.

MASON
Thanks, Jake. That means a lot to me.

TREW
[walkie talkie]
That's two guns down. You boys only got two more to
go.

JAKE
Whoa! Oh well, we'll have to keep moving down here.

MASON
Yeah, we'll find another way up.

JAKE
Look, there are some Metal Creatures waiting for us.
Should I use my new Powers to send them all away,
buddy?

MASON
It's up to you, Jake. You can use your new Powers
whenever you like.

JAKE
That's what I like to hear... Oh, hello, boys! And
goodbye... Come, Mason.

MASON
Whoa, there's the third gun, Jake! I think I should stay
here.

JAKE
Okay. I'll be right back.

TREW
[walkie talkie]
You just got one more gun to go. I'm really happy with
you boys.

JAKE
Thanks, Trew. We're doing great so far.

TREW
[walkie talkie]
That's good. Just keep on moving, boys. I'll see you
back here soon.

MASON
Hey, we've got more Metal Creatures in our way, Jake.

JAKE
Don't worry, Mason: I'll deal with them with this
sword.

MASON
And goodbye, you punks.

JAKE
There's the last gun, Mason. I'll deal with this one.

MASON
Hey, wait up, Jake. I'm coming with you.

TREW
[walkie talkie]
Nice work, boys. Come back to my place, I have
another mission for you.

JAKE
Okay, Trew. We're on our way back right now.

MASON
And we're back!

TREW
Nice work in the sewers. I'm really happy with your
work so far. So happy, in fact, that I have a contract for
you both.

JAKE
What's with the contact, Trew?

TREW
This contract is for a big race that I signed you up for. I
have a good friend that needs some good racers... If
you boys are up to it, that is.

MASON
I think we can do a race, Trew. We might be good
racers.

TREW
Good, because she said you two can be a team in the
race together. Just try not to get in any trouble at the
stadium.

MASON
Right.

TREW
I knew I could count on you boys. Now you need to get
a move on.

JAKE
Let's go, Mason.

MASON
I'm right behind you, Jake.

JAKE
Yes, we made it.

MASON.
Good. Let's go and see this friend of Trew's.

JAKE
Uh, hello? We're here to talk about the races…

***

ZORN
[walkie talkie]
Jake, Mason: I need you guys to come back to my
place.

JAKE
Okay, Zorn, we'll be there soon.

ZORN
I need you guys to go save an old friend of mine.
There's a portal there that might be of interest to you.

JAKE
You got it, Zorn. And what's your friend's name?

ZORN
His name is Dim, though I usually call him "the
brains."

MASON
And where is he hiding?

ZORN
He's hiding in the strip mine. There are Metal
Creatures there, too, so be careful when you guys get
there.

JAKE
Oh, I think we'll be just fine at the strip mine. We'll
take down all those Metal Creatures with this.

ZORN
That's a nice sword that you got there, Jake.

JAKE
Thanks, it's a gift from Trew for the last time we were
playing with the Metal Creatures.

ZORN
Better hurry, Dim doesn't like those Metal Creatures.

JAKE
You can count on us, Zorn. Let's go, Mason.

MASON
I'm right behind you, Jake.

JAKE
Well, here we are.

MASON
Wow, this place is awesome! Can we stay for a little
while? Please?

JAKE
Sorry, buddy, we really need to save Dim right now.
Maybe after we're done with him we can hang around
for a little while.

MASON
Okay. Let's do this thing.

JAKE
Whoa, look at this place!

MASON
I can see, Jake. This is the strip mine all right... Hey,
Jake, we've got some Metal Creatures coming down the
mountain.

JAKE
Don't worry, Mason, I can see the door.

DIM
Ah! Stay back!

MASON
Do something, Jake! This guy's crazy!

JAKE
Hey, are you Dim? We're here to help you. Zorn sent
us.

DIM
Stay back! I will shoot you! Wait, what? Friends? Good!
So, uh, where's the army?

MASON
Umm, we're it.

DIM
What? Just you two? What do they think I'm worth!

JAKE
I'm starting to think that myself. Now, you can stay
here and be Metal Creature lunch, but we're getting out
of here before those things make it down the mountain.

***

DIM
Hey, I wanted to thank you guys for saving my butt out there at the strip mine...

MASON
And we wanted to thank you for trying to shoot us back there.

DIM
Oh, yeah... I'm sorry about that, guys. I get jumpy sometimes.

MASON
You get jumpy. Dim, how can you get jumpy with Metal Creatures attacking you!

DIM
I don't usually, but sometimes I do. I don't wanna talk about it right now. We need to keep this shield wall up. If it goes down, we can kiss our butts goodbye.

JAKE
I've got a few surprises for those Metal Creatures.

DIM
Hold on there, Jake. We've got to keep the shield walls up until our leader determines our next step. But before he does that, we need to find out what Baron Hax is doing with the Metal Creatures. So I need you guys to go through this portal, where you'll arrive at The Platform. See how many Metal Creature eggs you can destroy there.

JAKE
Okay, Dim. We can do that for you. Let's go, Mason.

MASON
I'm right behind you, Jake... Whoa! This place is a little scary.

JAKE
I think it's okay, Mason. We just have to destroy all the Metal Creature eggs that we can find, like Dim said.

MASON
And how are we going to destroy all of those Metal Creature eggs, Jake?

JAKE
Oh, I think I see a little something that can help with our little problem... Oh yeah, let's do this thing.

MASON
This is amazing, Jake. Just you and me, destroying these Metal Creature eggs with this big gun, here.

JAKE
You can say that again, buddy.

MASON
It's just like the old days.

JAKE
You are a true friend, Mason.

MASON
Only five more eggs left, Jake.

DIM
Yes! You guys did it! With their eggs gone, there won't be any more Metal Creatures at the strip mine for a while.

JAKE
You're welcome, Dim. Always happy to help.

DIM
Oh, I am happy to hear that, Jake. I'm all set here for

now, though. Thanks.

ZORN
[walkie talkie]
Hey, I need you guys to come back here. I have another
mission for you.

JAKE
Okay, Zorn. We're on our way

GUARD 64
This is 64, we're en route.

GUARD 309
Nothing so far...

ZORN
An old friend from the guards is out at the water
station. Tells me the Metal Creatures are getting bigger
and stronger. Head on down there and see if she needs
any help.

JAKE
Did you say "she," Zorn?

ZORN
Don't ask. Stop that, Mason.

MASON
Okay, Zorn. Sorry about that.

ZORN
I need you guys to focus for this one. Now get going.

JAKE
You can count on us. Let's go, Mason.

MASON
I'm right behind you, Jake.

GUARD 1777
I hate the smell of this part of the City.

JAKE
And here we are. At the water station again, Mason.

MASON
Oh, great. How many times are we gonna have to come
here?

JAKE
Who knows, maybe this will be our last time.

MASON
Let's hope so, Jake.

JAKE
Hello, boys… And goodbye.

MASON
Nice shot, Jake. And what are we even doing here?
Risking our butts for some guard…

TAMMY
Who the heck are you two?

MASON
Oh wow, I really like girls that are in the guard
business. Sorry to interrupt, but my name is Mason,
and that is my friend Jake, and we are good friends.

TAMMY
Keep talking, Mason, and I'll shoot you and your
friend.

JAKE
Easy. Zorn asked us to help you.

TAMMY
I don't need any help, but you might. We got company.
Here they come!

MASON
Hey, Jake, there's one coming from the top!

JAKE
I got him, Mason. Thanks, buddy.

MASON
No problem.

TAMMY
Would you guys mind shutting up and fighting these
Creatures?

JAKE
Man, this girl really doesn't like us.

MASON
Yeah, I have to agree with you, Jake.

JAKE
Let's just keep on fighting.

MASON
Oh yeah! That's one less Metal Creature that we took
down... Hey, lady, I think we got off on the wrong foot
there, I'm...

TAMMY
Tell Zorn that Baron Hax is planning something, and it
might have to do with that thing.

JAKE
What is it?

TAMMY
It's some kind of key, opens a strange door.

JAKE
Your name is Tammy, huh?

TAMMY
We're even now. Maybe I'll see you boys again.

MASON
Whoa. I think I might be in love with that girl, Jake.

JAKE
Yeah, maybe not. She didn't seem that interested in us,
buddy.

MASON
Yeah, but I think maybe we can be friends with her,
especially if she's friends with Zorn from back when
they worked for Baron Hax.

JAKE
Maybe. Let's just get back to the City.

***

TREW
[walkie talkie]
Jake, Mason: I need you guys to come back to my place
and do a little mission for me.

JAKE
Okay, Trew. We're on our way.

GUARD 40
Be advised, I'm on foot.

GUARD 2319
Let me know if you see anything, dude.

GUARD 40
Don't worry, I will let you know.

MASON
Hello there. Are you new here? Hey, wait a second, I
know you... You're with Zorn!

HESSY
Shut up, please. My name is Hessy. And yes, I am with
Zorn, but he wants me to spy on Trew. I'll be here a
while, and no, I don't mind you talking to me.

MASON
Do you need any help back here?

HESSY
Umm, no thanks. Maybe later.

TREW
Hey, Jake, I need you and Mason to go out and collect
some items for me.

JAKE
No problem, Trew. We like to help you.

TREW
Oh, and be careful out there, boys. The guards might be
interested in those items, too.

MASON
Okay, Trew. We'll be careful. You can count on us.

GUARD 7878
Hey, guys, look: it's Jake and Mason. I think they are
doing something for Trew, guys.

GUARD 214
That's cool, dude. Just keep on looking for some more
stuff to do.

GUARD 7878
You got it. I'm on my way right now.

GUARD 590
Shut up, you guys. Just do your jobs before Baron Hax
destroys us all.

GUARD 7878
Sorry about that, dude.

GUARD 590
Thank you. Nothing like having dumb friends around.

MASON
We've got five items so far, Jake. Just need five more...
I'll let you know if I see any more from back here.

GUARD 7878
Nothing so far...

GUARD 214
I think Jake and Mason are almost done, you guys.

GUARD 7878
Yeah, I think you're right, dude... Let's just keep going.

GUARD 214
You got it, dude.

MASON
Man, Jake, none of these guards are coming to get us like Trew said they would.

JAKE
Well, that's a good thing.

GUARD 999
Hey, guys, sorry I'm late. I had to take my kids to the park today.

GUARD 590
It's good to see you, dude. How was the park?

GUARD 999
It was fun. My kids had a great time. They're with their mom now.

GUARD 590
That's cool. We need your help to find more jobs now.

GUARD 999
You got it, dude.

JAKE
That's all of them, Mason. We've got all ten items. Let's head back to Trew.

TREW
Nice work getting those items for me, boys. Now I need you guys to leave, please. It's time for me to rest.

MASON
Okay, Trew. We will let you rest. Just let us know if you
need anything else.

TREW
Sure thing, Mason.

***

JAKE
Come on, Mason, let's go see that new guy Tammy was
telling us about.

MASON
Okay, Jake. I'm right behind you.

GUARD 196
Moving to the next wave point...

GUARD 116
Do you need any help on your next wave point?

GUARD 196
No thanks, I'm pretty good right now.

GUARD 116
Just let me know if you need any help, dude.

GUARD 196
You got it.

MASON
Cool. Check out all the dead stuff. Ow!

BECKER
Put your hand on me again, little boy, and you'll be
counting with your feet. I am Becker. This is my friend,
Carson.

CARSON
Hello there, I am Carson. Becker there is my best
friend. Yeah, I know his name is a little funny.

BECKER
Yes, it's a little funny. But enough about my name.
We're glad to finally meet you guys.

CARSON
Yeah, it's good see you again, Jake.

JAKE
But... We never met before, Carson.

CARSON
I know. But I've still known you for a long time. You,
too, Mason.

MASON
How do you know me, Carson?

CARSON
I just know everyone that's new here in LA. And I
heard you've wanted to live here for a long time.

BECKER
Is that true, Mason? Do you really want to live here in
LA?

MASON
Yes, it is true. I've always wanted to live in LA.

JAKE
Umm... Sorry to interrupt, but... How old are you,
Carson?

CARSON
I am eight years old. I want to stay as a little boy for a
long time.

MASON
Hey, I want to stay as a seven year-old! I think I just
made a new friend, Jake.

BECKER
You can be friends after you go out in the forest and

find three items for us.

CARSON
Yeah, Becker is right. We need you guys to go out there
and find three items for us. Not two, not four. Three.

BECKER
Be free to do whatever you want after that mission.

JAKE
Don't worry, Carson and Becker. We'll find them.

CARSON
Yeah, they will definitely be our friends. What do you
think, Becker?

BECKER
Yes, I agree, Carson. I think he's even wearing
underwear already... Unlike you.

CARSON
Yeah, but I think he's considering wearing diapers
again, like me.

BECKER
You never know.

GUARD 40
Do you need any help?

GUARD 845
No thanks, I'm good for now. Maybe later, dude.

GUARD 40
Okay. Just asking.

GUARD 845
Yeah, I know.

GUARD 2319
[walkie talkie]
En route to the next wave point.

JAKE
Well, this is the place, Mason.

MASON
Wow! This place is pretty cool, Jake.

JAKE
Let's just go find that stuff for Becker and Carson.

MASON
Okay, Jake. I'm right behind you... I think that's one of
the items! I'll get it... Only two more to go... Oh crap!
Look at that giant rhino Metal Creature!

JAKE
Let me handle this thing, Mason... It's gone now.

MASON
Wow, another easy item. I think this mission is really
awesome... We should thank Carson and Becker when
we're done here, Jake.

JAKE
You do that. I just want to find the last one...

MASON
Watch out for the rockslide... There's the last item!
This one's pretty heavy. I might need your help with it.

JAKE
Don't worry, I'll get it.

BECKER
Nice work, guys. I think we can be friends now.

CARSON
Yay! You're free from us now. We'll let you know if we
need anything else.

JAKE
We'll see you guys later... Hey, Mason, we should go
ask Dim for a little help with something.

MASON
Okay.

JAKE
Dim, buddy, we need your help.

DIM
I cannot help with your new Powers.

JAKE
We just need your help to get up to Baron Hax's tower.
Maybe you can unlock the door for us.

DIM
Yeah, I think I can try to help you guys out. But I'll
need you guys to destroy the gun emplacements
outside first so I can get over to the elevator.

JAKE
Thanks, Dim. We owe you one.

DIM
I like that you guys are my friends.

MASON
Yeah, we're almost friends, Dim. Soon. We'll talk to you
when we're done.

GUARD 64
Hey guys, look: Jake and Mason are destroying the

guns for us. Do you think we should help them out?

GUARD 196
If you want to help them, dude, knock yourself out.

GUARD 309
Hey, come on, guys. I think we should all help them
out. Get every guard to take a shot at one of the last
three guns.

GUARD 64
You heard 309, guys. Destroy them for Jake and
Mason. Now!

GUARD 196
You got it, 64.

GUARD 7878
Patrolling Area-9.

GUARD 64
We need your help on destroying the last gun, dude.

GUARD 7878
I'm on my way.

DIM
Nice work, fellows. See you soon.

JAKE
It looks likes the guards aren't trying to stop us. I think
they're helping us.

MASON
And is that a good thing, Jake?

JAKE
Yes, it is a good thing, Mason. We've only got three left,

and...

MASON
Good, great, let's do this fast because I need to get going.

JAKE
What do you mean, Mason?

MASON
I need to go, Jake.

JAKE
Oh, okay. Let's finish this up, then we can find a bathroom.

DIM
Nice work, guys. I already opened the elevator door to Baron Hax's tower. I'll let you guys know if I need you for anything later.

JAKE
Okay. Thanks, Dim. We'll talk to you later. Come on, Mason, let's go find a bathroom for you.

GUARD 214
Right, we'll check it out.

JAKE
Hey, Mason, I see the boys' room.

MASON
Oh, good. Please wait out here, Jake. I'll be quick.

GUARD 999
Smells around here.

GUARD 309
Sorry I'm late, guys.

GUARD 590
Where have you been, 309?

GUARD 309
I was busy with some Metal Creatures at the water
station.

GUARD 999
Oh man, dude, tell us more...

MASON
Okay, Jake. All done.

JAKE
Let's head up to Baron Hax's tower now, buddy.

MASON
Whoa! I don't think this is safe, Jake.

JAKE
It's okay, Mason. Just hop on my back and I can carry
you again... Now we need to stay quiet...

BARON HAX
You know I still don't have enough Power for you,
William. I'll have what I owe you next week.

WILLIAM
I hope so, Baron. Otherwise, I might have a problem
with you and your men.

DRYAN
He's playing with us, Baron. We need to move on to the
new plan now.

BARON HAX
Hold on, Dryan. I know you're mad, but we can't move on with the new plan until we find our new friend. Call Tammy for me, please.

DRYAN
But your daughter doesn't have the time to help us out with those Metal Creatures.

JAKE
Tammy is Baron Hax's daughter?

BARON HAX
I need you to find the child, too, Dryan. And avoid that girl at the racetrack.

DRYAN
As you wish, sir.

MASON
Jake, what are they talking about?

JAKE
Quiet!

DRYAN
What was that?

JAKE
Uh oh, they know we're here.

BARON HAX
Oh, hey, guys. I have been looking everywhere for you two. I was thinking we can have a fun fight together.

JAKE
Uh... Okay, Baron Hax. We can have a fun fight right now.

BARON HAX
Thanks, Jake. I'll go easy you boys... You won the fight!
Good job. See you guys later.

MASON
Yeah, I don't think we're going to see each other again
anytime soon. Bye bye.

***

JAKE
Feels good to be back in the City.

MASON
Yeah, I didn't like it in that tower.

JAKE
I think Zorn needs us again. Let's go see him.

ZORN
This City is on high alert! What the heck did you guys
do?

MASON
Us? Nothing! We were just taking a stroll through the
City.

ZORN
Really. Then why are the guards looking for a
seventeen year-old with brown hair and a seven year-
old boy with a backpack full of underwear?

MASON
Umm, I'm not sure. Leave my underwear out of this.

JAKE
Look, we climbed to Baron Hax's tower and maybe
tripped a few alarms.

MASON
Oh, yeah. That, too.

ZORN
What! I didn't give you orders to do that.

JAKE
Hey, Baron Hax was nice to us. He just wanted to have
a fun fight.

MASON
And we overheard him talking to a guy named William.

CARCOSA CADEN
You saw William? The leader of the Metal Creatures?

JAKE
No, he was on some kind of screen. But we heard him
talking to Baron Hax.

MASON
Baron Hax is thinking of bringing some new Powers to
William.

CARCOSA CADEN
Hmm. It will never be enough.

MASON
But William might double-cross Baron Hax soon.

CARCOSA CADEN
Is that so? Maybe Hax will be of some help fighting the
Metal Creatures after all.

JAKE
Why didn't you tell me Tammy was Baron Hax's
daughter?

ZORN
Because it was none of your business. Now, I need you
guys to help my men move to a new hideout. Don't
mess this up, Jake.

CARCOSA CADEN
Do you think they can do it, Zorn?

ZORN
I hope so. Just keep an eye on the kid.

MASON
There are Zorn's men.

GAGE
Thanks for coming, you guys. Let's get a move on...

GUARD 2319
Hey, look: I think Jake and Mason are doing another
mission for Zorn.

GUARD 64
Do you want to help them out?

GUARD 590
Nah, we have our own things to do.

ZORN
Nice work, guys. Our operation can continue. Come on
back to the hideout.

GUARD 1777
Moving to the next area...

ZORN
Metal Creatures are lining up outside the City.

MASON
What happened to Baron Hax fighting them?

ZORN
His guards were fighting them, but very few made it
back. To meet our leader, he'd appreciate...

JAKE
You want us to back out there and finish up the job.
Let's go, Mason.

MASON
Man, I still get bad dreams about this place.

JAKE
Let's just get this over with.

MASON
Wait... Is that? No, it can't be...

JAKE
It's... Sammy's house.

MASON
But how, Jake?

JAKE
I think this place is our home.

MASON
We need to find Sammy!

JAKE
Come on, Mason. Let's head back to Zorn's place first.

ZORN
Our leader's decided that it's time to meet you guys.

JAKE
Why's that place out there so important to you, Zorn?

ZORN
I'll let you know once I've had a chance to investigate
that old house.

JAKE
We used to know who lived there...

SAMMY 2
So you're the guys that keep getting into trouble.

MASON
Sammy! Is that you?

SAMMY 2
Welcome to our team. I am our leader. And you are?

MASON
Wait. Sammy, do you remember us?

SAMMY 2
I'm sorry, kid. I've never seen you before.

JAKE
Come on, Sammy, it's us. Jake and Mason. We came through the portal with you, and Emma, and your friend Bryan...

MASON
Yeah! We've been looking for you and Emma forever, Sammy. Now we can go find your daughter...

SAMMY 2
Listen, boys, I don't know what kind of crap you have been eating, but I don't have time for this. We have a war to win, and a child to save. Besides, I don't really like going through portals.

MASON
It sounds like Sammy, Jake...

JAKE
Yeah, but it's not the Sammy we're used to, buddy.

SAMMY 2
You guys have been doing well in your missions for

Zorn. But now I have a task for you: I need you to go out to the forest and destroy as many Metal Creatures as you can.

MASON

JAKE
Alright, Mason, let's go deal with those Metal Creatures.

MASON
I'm right behind you, Jake.

JAKE
Well, here we are again.

MASON
Oh, great. I don't like this place, Jake. Can I hang on your back again, please?

JAKE
Sure, Mason, you can hold onto me... Wait. Is that our jetboard?

MASON
Jake, use the jetboard to catch up to those Metal Creatures!

JAKE
Got them!

SAMMY 2
[walkie talkie]
Nice work, boys. I think you're finally starting to become heroes. If I need anything else from you guys, I'll let you know.

TREW
[walkie talkie]
Jake, Mason, this is Trew: I need you boys to take care

of some bombs floating in my waters. Baron Hax placed them there to stop Metal Creatures, but they're getting in the way. Get to them with your jetboard and disarm them.

JAKE
Don't worry, Trew. We're almost there... Whoa, look at them all... Let's see what we can do.

TREW
Good work, boys. I'm really happy with your work so far. Perhaps we can be friends soon.

JAKE
Come on, Mason. Let's head to Trew's place.

TREW
Sorry about that, boys. Guards are always coming in here, talking non-stop and asking for favors. I need you boys to go free some monsters.

MASON
Wait, monsters? I don't like monsters.

JAKE
Don't worry, buddy, I'll be with you.

MASON
Thanks, Jake. I'm glad to have a true friend like you.

TREW
There are three monsters. Be careful bringing them to my friend Haden.

JAKE
You can count on us.

GUARD 116
Hello there! We heard that you guys are going to save
these here monsters.

JAKE
Yeah. Are you guys going to run away when we free
them?

GUARD 40
Yes, we are going to run away from these monsters.

MASON
Come on, big guys, let's rock.

JAKE
Are you Haden?

HADEN
Yes. You guys saved my friends for me. Thank you.

MASON
Uh, you're welcome, Haden. Umm, no offense, but you
kind of scare me.

HADEN
I heard you don't like monsters, eh?

JAKE
Haden, we have to go now. We'll see you later.

***

TREW
You know, boys, I always miss being an art collector, because now I'm a trophy collector. I have a new dream.

MASON
We all have dreams, Trew.

TREW
Yes, but this is me we're talking about now. Have I ever told you boys about my statue of... Oh, I don't remember his name...

JAKE
Umm, no. You haven't.

TREW
Well, he was a great hero back in the day. My best men got it for me. It had a ruby key. But both it and my men got flushed away.

JAKE
I'm sorry, Trew.

TREW
No matter, I need you boys to go back down to the sewers and get that ruby key for me.

JAKE
Great. More fun in the mud.

MASON
That's not mud down there, buddy.

GUARD 590
Patrolling Area 5.

MASON
Oh, great. We're back in the sewers again.

JAKE
You wanna hop on my back again, Mason?

MASON
Yeah, sure... I think that's the statue, Jake. I'll get the key... Whoa!

JAKE
Got it! Where would you be without me?

MASON
Well, Jake, I think I might be acting for a studio, and singing, and maybe getting diapers for myself, instead of being knee-deep in muck. Man, I miss diapers.

JAKE
Well, maybe we can find a store that has diapers, and you can buy some.

MASON
Let's hope so.

GUARD 2319
999, are you coming to my position soon, dude?

GUARD 999
[walkie talkie]
Sorry, 2319. I'll see you on break. Meet me at my favorite pizza place, dude.

GUARD 2319
You got it, dude. I'll see you there.

SAMMY 2
[walkie talkie]
Jake, Mason: this is Sammy. I need you boys to come back to the hideout for a minute, please.

JAKE
Okay, Sammy. We're on our way back now.

SAMMY 2
I want you boys to take this kid to Caden for me. I just don't have the time to watch him today.

JAKE
So what's this kid's story?

SAMMY 2
I found him playing in the streets by himself.

MASON
Oh, um, okay. Don't worry, Sammy. You can count on us.

JAKE
Hey, kid, wait! Come back!

GUARD 1777
Hey, look: it's Jake and Mason again. They're taking that kid to Caden. Should we follow them?

GUARD 309
I don't think so, 1777. We'll probably see them soon.

GUARD 1777
Sorry, I was just asking.

GUARD 309
It's okay.

JAKE
Stay with me, kid, and you'll be fine.

MASON
Sammy told us to take the kid to you.

CARCOSA CADEN
Thank you for sending him to me, boys. I have enjoyed
watching over him.

JAKE
Yeah, I'm sure. I'm pretty good with kids, too.

MASON
I think we need to go now, Jake.

CARCOSA CADEN
Wait. Before you leave, I have something for you.

JAKE
What is it, Caden?

CARCOSA CADEN
It'll allow you access to a secret cave. William has a
weapon-like machine in there that must be destroyed.

MASON
Okay, we can do that... Uh, Jake? Is it okay if I ride on
your back again?

JAKE
Sure, Mason.

MASON
Thanks, Jake.

TAMMY
Hello, guys. What brings you here?

JAKE
Tammy... What are you doing here?

TAMMY
Just trying to figure out how to destroy this machine.

MASON
Hey, we're here to do the same thing.

TAMMY
Really? Glad to see you're eager to help out. Sorry for
being so rude when we first met.

JAKE
It's okay, Tammy.

TAMMY
And you guys know that Baron Hax is my father...

JAKE
Yeah, we overheard when we went to his tower. He
wanted to fun fight us.

TAMMY
Yeah, my dad likes to have fun fights with people. He
doesn't like to go hardball.

MASON
Yeah, we sort of figured that out.

TAMMY
Okay, less chatting, more destroying.

JAKE
You got it, Tammy.

GUARD 116
Hey, why are those guys down there destroying the
machine?

GUARD 590
I think they're trying to stop William's evil plans.

GUARD 40
Should we help them?

GUARD 590
We should most definitely help them. Let's go, men.

MASON
Uh, Jake? I think we've got some guards helping us
out.

TAMMY
My father only hires good guards.

GUARD 590
Okay, here's the plan: we stay and deal with the anchor
ropes up here. Those guys will deal with the ropes
down there.

GUARD 40
Got it.

GUARD 116
How are we gonna do this?

GUARD 590
Leave that to me, dude.

GUARD 116
Oh, okay. I get it now.

GUARD 590
See, I told you.

CARCOSA CADEN
[walkie talkie]
Nice work, boys. I think you boys are starting to
become fine heroes. I'll let you know if I need anything
else.

TAMMY
Thanks for the help, guys.

JAKE
No problem, Tammy. I'm sure we'll help each other
again soon.

TAMMY
You said it, Jake.

BECKER
Oh! Hey, guys. What brings you here?

JAKE
Hey, Becker, Carson. What are you guys doing here?

CARSON
I just wanted to go for a walk with Becker and see what
kind of stuff they have here in LA. Hey, Mason, do you
want to wear diapers again?

MASON
Yes, I do, Carson. I do want to wear diapers again. Why
do you ask?

CARSON
Just wondering.

BECKER
Wow, I guess he really does want to wear diapers again.
I wouldn't have known. Anyways, I'm afraid we have to
go now. We'll see you guys again.

JAKE
Okay. Bye, guys. We'll see you around.

CARSON
Okay. We'll see you later.

TAMMY
Hello, boys.

BECKER
Oh. Hello, Tammy. What brings you here?

TAMMY
I was just out in the mountains dealing with the bomb
machine. With a little help from Jake, Mason, and the
guards, of course.

CARSON
Wow, that's awesome. The machine is out of the
picture now?

TAMMY
Yes, Carson. Well, I need to go now.

BECKER
Okay, we'll see you later, Tammy.

MASON
Time to go tell the girl at the racetrack we don't want to
do her dumb race.

***

JAKE
...And then we destroyed the machine out in a
mountain cave.

EMMA
That's really cool, but I can't talk to you guys right now.
I need you to leave.

JAKE
Are you always this uncool?

MASON
Let me handle this, Jake. Listen, lady. We're done
doing everything you say.

EMMA
Wait... That voice...

MASON
And another thing: we don't want to do your dumb
race. Let's go, Jake.

EMMA
Mason... It is you!

MASON
Emma?

EMMA
I've been looking everywhere for you guys! It's been
such a long time. And Jake, you look, uh, different.

JAKE
It's been a long time.

MASON
Baron Hax gave our friend here some new Powers, and
they gave him a chance to talk now.

EMMA
I think that portal brought us to Los Angeles. And I know that's your dream place, Mason, but I don't think I really like it here.

JAKE
We also found your dad... Well, kind of.

MASON
He seems kind of different. Thinks he's the leader of some resistance team.

JAKE
You need to go see him when you have the chance.

EMMA
I've been working on a new car to get us out of here. Jake, we really need to leave. I don't like this place at all. The people scare me.

TREW
Jake, my boy. I need that ruby key from the sewers!

JAKE
Sorry about that, Trew. I kind of forgot about that.

EMMA
Hey, there's gonna be a big race soon. You could still join up with my team, if you wanted to...

JAKE
Uh, sure, Emma. We can join your race team.

MASON
Umm, Jake? Is it okay if I stay here with Emma?

JAKE
Sure, Mason. You can stay here with Emma.

MASON
Umm, Emma, this is our new friend Trew. Trew, this is
our good friend Emma. We've known her for a very
long time.

TREW
Oh, I know, we've met before. She's a good friend of
mine, too.

EMMA
It's good to see you again, Trew. I see you are having
Jake and Mason work for you.

TREW
Yeah, these boys are pretty awesome.

EMMA
They're awesome friends, and they'll do anything you
ask of them.

ANNOUNCER
Attention racers: the first race is about to begin!

MASON
Sounds like the race is about to start, Emma. Think
Jake will be able to win the race for us?

EMMA
Yeah, I think he's got what it takes.

TREW
Well, I need to go now, Mason. I'll see you and Jake
soon.

MASON
Okay, Trew. See you later.

EMMA
He seems like a nice guy, Mason.

MASON
Yeah. Trew is nice to us.

JAKE
Yes! I won, guys.

MASON
That's cool, Jake. I knew you could do it, buddy.

EMMA
You did great, Jake. Just two more races to go.

MASON
And I'm doing the next one.

TAMMY
Hey, I saw you race tonight.

JAKE
Really? Was I any good?

TAMMY
Yeah, you were, Jake.

JAKE
Oh, sorry. Umm, Emma, this is Tammy. She's a friend.

EMMA
Nice to meet you, Tammy.

TAMMY
Nice to meet you, too.

JAKE
And this is Emma. She's is a really good friend of mine.

TAMMY
I can see that, Jake. I just wanted to let you know I'm
heading out to do a mission with the guards. You're
free to join us, if you'd like.

JAKE
Yeah, sure, Tammy. We like helping out.

TAMMY
Alright. I'm heading out, then.

JAKE
Okay. We'll be there soon.

MASON
Sorry about that, Emma. Tammy is a little hard with
us. She's an okay friend.

EMMA
It's okay, Mason. I know what you mean. I'll try to be
friends with her.

JAKE
Yeah. I think you might be friends with her soon,
Emma. But we need to get a move on. Let's go, Mason.

MASON
I'm right behind you, Jake.

JAKE
We'll see you soon, Emma.

EMMA
I'm gonna see if I can find my dad.

GUARD 196
Nothing so far...

MASON
Hey, Tammy, I see you brought your boys with you.

TAMMY
Jake, Mason. I knew I could count on you.

JAKE
You know we can't say no to a Metal Creature party.

TAMMY
I hope you're ready, because here they come.

MASON
Ahhh! A Metal Creature sneak attack!

GUARD 196
Gah!

TAMMY
Darn it. It's just us now. Help me take them all out.

JAKE
I'm trying to, there's just too many of them.

TAMMY
Almost done... Yes! That's all of them. Good work,
guys. Thanks for the help.

JAKE
You're welcome, Tammy.

MASON
Okay, now that that's done, let's go see if anyone else
needs us.

***

DIM
Jake! We still have trouble at the strip mine. I think
Baron Hax has set me up. No, wait... I think everybody
is trying to get me.

JAKE
What are you talking about, Dim?

DIM
Metal Creatures are coming out of those Power wells. I
think it's making them... It just doesn't make any
sense... You know, the Power wells that keep the shield
walls up. These bombs should do the trick. Just drop
one into each well. The blast should do the rest... Hey,
be careful with that!

MASON
I mean, I'm sure we can do this mission, but... How do
these bombs work? Ah! Um, I believe these are yours.

DIM
Hey, not my problem anymore.

MASON
No, really. This is yours, Dim.

DIM
Hey, you're the hero, Mason.

MASON
No, Jake's the hero... Oops, my bad...

DIM
Great. Now you've bombed the whole thing. Don't
move... On second thought, move. Far away. Now. Go
through the portal and drop the rest of the bombs in
the wells. You've only got a few minutes...

MASON
Yes! That's all of them. Let's get out of here. This place kind of scares me, Jake.

JAKE
Okay, Mason. We'll head out now.

DIM
Yes! All the wells have been destroyed. Thanks for the help, guys. I owe you one.

MASON
Poor Dim. I feel so sorry for him. He's really scared of Metal Creatures.

CARCOSA CADEN
For good reason, too. Dim got too close to one as a boy, and now he never goes outside.

MASON
Wow. That does explain why he's always hanging out in this place.

CARCOSA CADEN
I'm sure he will come back outside when all the Metal Creatures are gone.

MASON
Well, let's hope so, because we really want Dim to come outside with us... Hey, uh, Caden? Is everything okay?

CARCOSA CADEN
Yeah, everything's good. I was just thinking about something. Nothing you'd understand.

MASON
Oh. Okay.

CARCOSA CADEN
Anyways, I need you guys to head back to The Platform
and take care of that Big Ship. It's up to no good.

MASON
Don't worry, Caden. You can count on us.

GUARD 7878
Oh, hey, guys. Are you here to help out with that Big
Ship?

JAKE
Yes, we are.

GUARD 2319
Good. We need all the help we can get.

GUARD 845
We'll go on ahead. You guys take care of that big gun.

JAKE
Okay. We've got the big gun.

GUARD 7878
I think those boys are really nice.

GUARD 2319
Of course they're nice, dude.

GUARD 7878
I know that, dude. Just trying to lighten the mood.

GUARD 845
Less talking, more shooting.

GUARD 7878
You're right. Let's do this thing together.

MASON
Yes! The Big Ship is gone.

GUARD 7878
Thank you, boys. We couldn't have destroyed the Big
Ship without your help.

MASON
You're welcome. We like to help out a lot.

GUARD 2319
This is 2319, we're en route...

***

MASON
So there I was, a two-on-one fight with these Metal
Creatures. I kind of ran away a little bit, but I decided
to go back and fight them again. And when there was
only one Metal Creature left, I jumped on top of it! And
made it go all crazy! And then boom! The Metal
Creature was down and out.

HESSY
Wow, Mason. You are so awesome.

KIG
Yeah, sounds like you're the guy for my next mission.
Saw three Metal Creatures wandering the forest. Go
take care of them, and you can tell us all about it when
you get back.

MASON
Don't worry, Kig. We'll do our best.

GUARD 590
Searching for suspects...

GUARD 999
Do you want to get some food after your shift, dude?

GUARD 590
Sure, 999. We can get some food when I'm done.

MASON
Wow, Jake. It was nice riding on your back while you
took down those Metal Creatures.

KIG
Nice work, boys, I knew you could do it. You boys are
starting to become true heroes.

GUARD 590
Right, we'll check it out.

SAMMY 2
The three of us were just talking about you, Jake.
Carson was very pleased with what you did.

JAKE
What we did?

BECKER
Yes. We are very happy with your hard work, guys.

MASON
Did you have something else for us, Carson?

CARSON
I have something that needs to be done, but it might be
a little hard.

JAKE
Whatever it is, we can try.

CARSON
I just need you to go back to the mountain cave and
grab something for me.

SAMMY 2
More and more Metal Creatures are showing up there.
We're not sure why, so you need to be careful.

BECKER
Hopefully we'll find out why soon.

JAKE
You want us to head back there right now?

CARSON
Yes, Jake.

JAKE
Okay, Carson. We'll do our best. Let's go, Mason.

MASON
I'm on it.

GUARD 64
Right. We'll check it out.

GUARD 214
Do you need any help, 64?

GUARD 116
Yeah, me and 214 are just walking around doing
nothing.

GUARD 64
Uh, no thanks, guys. I'm good for now.

MASON
Whoa. This place is kind of scary.

JAKE
Hey, Mason, I've got an idea: I think you should hop in
my underwear. I'll be able to do this and have you with
me at the same time.

MASON
Umm. Thanks, Jake, but I think I'll just stick with
being on your back.

JAKE
Okay, whatever makes you happy, buddy. Just let me
know if you change your mind.

MASON
Okay, Jake. I will... Whoa! I think that's the statue
Carson was talking about. I'll get it, Jake.

JAKE
Be careful.

MASON
I will... Whoa! Jake, get it!

JAKE
Got it.

MASON
That was a close one... Hey, uh, Jake? Can you catch
me on my way down?

JAKE
Sure, buddy.

MASON
Thanks, Jake.

JAKE
No problem. Now let's get out of here.

MASON
I'm right behind you.

GUARD 309
Let us know when you get anything, dude.

GUARD 590
You got it, 309.

***

ZORN
Baron Hax is pleased with your progress. Whatever
you're doing, keep it up.

JAKE
I'm just doing my thing.

ZORN
He's brought in some yellow-suited guards, and they're
taking out my men. I need you to go out and destroy
their cars.

JAKE
If that's what you want me to do. Tell your men to be
more careful, though.

YELLOW GUARD ALPHA
Moving to Area-5.

GUARD 2319
Oh, hey, guys. Here for more fun?

JAKE
Yeah, Zorn wants us to blow up the yellow guards' cars.

YELLOW GUARD BETA
We'll be hard on you if you do, but I guess we don't
mind.

JAKE
Hey, don't worry about it. You guys can be hard on us,
if you want to.

YELLOW GUARD ALPHA
Hey, thanks. We'll try our best not to shoot you.

JAKE
Let's do this.

YELLOW GUARD GAMMA
How's it going, dude?

GUARD 7878
It's going good so far, dude. How about you?

YELLOW GUARD GAMMA
It's going good. Hey, can I walk with you?

GUARD 7878
Sure. You can walk with me.

YELLOW GUARD BETA
This is Yellow Beta, we're en route.

GUARD 116
I hate the smell of this part of the City.

GUARD 196
Is the smell really so bad?

GUARD 116
Yes. Why do you ask?

GUARD 196
No reason. I just wanted to ask.

ZORN
[walkie talkie]
Nice work, guys. If only I could've joined you.

YELLOW GUARD BETA
Patrolling Area-9...

CARCOSA CADEN
Looks like you guys will be great friends. Jake, Mason,
I think I'll stick around with you for a while. Sammy's
going to need our help.

BECKER
Come on in, guys. We were just chatting about our
plan, but now it's time to get a move on.

JAKE
Okay, Becker. What do you need from us?

CARSON
You guys need to open the secret door so the kid can do
his challenges.

CARCOSA CADEN
Do please hurry.

JAKE
Don't worry, Caden. We'll do our best.

MASON
Whoa, I think that's the statue we need to open the
secret door Carson told us about.

JAKE
I'll put the key in, and you push the button.

MASON
Okay, Jake. Let's do it.

JAKE
And... Now!

CARSON
Nice work, guys. We'll meet you inside.

JAKE
You got it, Carson.

CARSON
Hey, you guys made it in time.

JAKE
Told you we'd make it in time. So this is the door to the
kid's challenges?

SAMMY 2
Yes. He must do them on his own, and I'm sure he'll do
his very best.

BECKER
Umm, you guys, I don't think the kid can do these
challenges.

CARSON
Why, Becker?

BECKER
Because the kid needs to be a little older in order to do
these challenges.

SAMMY 2
Oh, great. So we brought the kid here for nothing.

JAKE
Don't worry, I think I should be the one to do these
challenges. Come on, Mason.

MASON
Umm, Jake, I don't think I want to do those challenges,
buddy.

JAKE
It's okay, Mason. Here, hop in my underwear.

MASON
Okay, Jake.

BECKER
Wait, guys! No! You can't!

SAMMY 2
No... They are going to do the challenges together.

CARCOSA CADEN
This was not part of the plan.

GUARD 7878
Hey, guys. We need you all to come with us, please.
Baron Hax wants to talk to you guys.

GUARD 999
We're sorry that we have to take you. We're just doing
our job.

SAMMY 2
I hope Jake and Mason can finish in time.

CARCOSA CADEN
Don't worry, Sammy. They will.

MASON
Whoa! This place is a little scary, Jake.

JAKE
Don't worry, Mason. You're safe in my underwear. I'll
do my challenge first, then you can do yours, buddy.

MASON
Okay, Jake. I'll wait in your underwear while you do
your thing. Wake me up when I can do mine.

JAKE
Okay, Mason. Time to do yours.

MASON
Okay, Jake. I'll meet you at the door when I'm done.

JAKE
Okay.

BARON HAX
Hey, guys. I see you are here to get the stone for Carson
and Becker. That's nice of you.

MASON
Umm, thanks, Baron Hax. What brings you here?

BARON HAX
I just felt like coming here and seeing if you two
wanted to have another fun fight.

JAKE
Uh, yeah. I think we have time for another fun fight
with you, Baron.

BARON HAX
Good. Also, I need to take the stone from you guys.
That's my mission.

JAKE
It's okay, Baron Hax. You can take the stone when
we're done.

BARON HAX
No! I lost again. Oh well. Thanks for another fun fight,
boys. I need to take the stone now. I'll see you boys
later.

***

JAKE
How did Baron Hax know about the stone?

ZORN
It's my fault. He would've done bad things to Tammy. I couldn't risk it.

MASON
Yeah, but now Baron Hax has the stone. He can do whatever he wants now.

ZORN
The only way to get the stone back, and to free our friends, is to head back to the prison.

JAKE
And why should we trust you after you talked to Hax?

ZORN
Aren't you listening? He would've done bad things to his own daughter. Guys, we just need to get to the prison. I need to grab Dim, and I'll meet you there.

JAKE
You just get that door open. We'll be there.

YELLOW GUARD GAMMA
I've been on duty for two days straight.

MASON
Whoa, we're back in this place again.

JAKE
Don't worry, Mason. We'll be quick.

MASON
Hey there, Hessy. We came to save you just in time.

HESSY
Hey, Jake, Mason. It's good to see you again.

JAKE
Sammy, are you okay?

SAMMY
It's about time you boys got here. My daughter and I
have been waiting forever. What happened to you,
Jake?

MASON
Wait, Sammy? Is that you?

SAMMY
Yes, it's me, Mason.

SAMMY 2
Oh. I see there's another me.

SAMMY
What do you mean by that?

SAMMY 2
Just that you look a bit like me. But not really.

MASON
Uh, okay. I'm kind of lost here.

JAKE
Dim, turn on the portal. Let's go, guys.

***

SAMMY
Three of Baron Hax's Robots have been set free.
They're catching up to his men.

SAMMY 2
And they're catching up fast.

SAMMY
Now the Robots are now on their way here. If any of
them get to this place, we're dead.

SAMMY 2
Hey, it's okay. We've got Jake and Mason for the job.

SAMMY
But can they make it in time?

SAMMY 2
Take out all three of the Robots before they reach the
hideout, Jake. It's all we've got.

SAMMY & SAMMY 2
Good hunting!

GUARD 196
There it is! Shoot it!

YELLOW GUARD ALPHA
I can see the Robot, men! Let's get it!

YELLOW GUARD GAMMA
Men, help those boys out!

GUARD 1777
Help out Jake and Mason!

GUARD 2319
Shoot that thing!

MASON
Yes! That's all of them, Jake. Let's go see Emma again.

JAKE
Okay, Mason. Let's go.

YELLOW GUARD BETA
Man, sewage duty sucks.

DRYAN
Well, if it isn't Jake and Mason...

JAKE
Where's Emma?

DRYAN
She's with her father.

EMMA
It's good to see you again, Dad.

SAMMY
It's been a long time, Emma. Now we just need to find
Bryan. I still don't know where he is.

DRYAN
I'll be sure to check out Mason's race after. I'll see you
guys later.

JAKE
Okay, Dryan. We'll see you later.

EMMA
Man, Dryan is a good friend.

JAKE
I'm glad that you're friends with him now, Emma.

EMMA
Where's Mason? He needs to get ready for his race.

MASON
Just let me put on my lucky underwear.

JAKE
You do that, Mason.

SAMMY
So you guys already got together before I found you.

JAKE
Umm, kind of, Sammy. Mason and I were working with Trew, and he told us about the race team. That's how we found Emma.

EMMA
I didn't know it was them at first, but then I heard Mason's voice.

SAMMY
Well, we still need to find Bryan. We'll do it together, as a team.

JAKE
You got it, Sammy. I'm sure Mason and I will be able to find him for you.

CARSON
Hey, Jake!

JAKE
Hey, Carson, Becker. What brings you guys here?

BECKER
We just wanted to come and see you race tonight, Jake.

JAKE
Oh. Sorry, Mason is gonna be racing tonight. You can stay around for that, if you want.

CARSON
Okay. We can stay and watch Mason race tonight.

BECKER
I think we should go find a seat, Carson. We'll see you later, Jake.

JAKE
Okay, Becker. We'll see you guys later.

ANNOUNCER
Attention, all racers: the second race is about to begin.

MASON
Okay, I think I'm ready to race now.

EMMA
Let's go, Mason! The race is about to begin!

MASON
Okay, Emma. I'm coming.

JAKE
Good luck, Mason! I'll be here waiting for you, buddy.

MASON
Okay, Jake. I'll do my best.

EMMA
Good luck, Mason!

MASON
Don't make this too easy for me, boys... Yes! I won the race!

EMMA
Mason! Over here, buddy.

MASON
Out of my way, you dorks. Eat my dust.

BECKER
Hey, Mason! You did good out there, buddy.

MASON
Thanks, Becker. It's good to see you guys again.

CARSON
We just wanted to see you race tonight, Mason.

SAMMY
I'm proud of you, Mason. You did your best out there.

MASON
Thanks, Sammy. That means a lot to me.

***

GUARD 214
Umm, sorry, dude. I'd love to help out, but I'm off my shift. Need to go see my kids now.

GUARD 64
Tell your kids I said hey.

GUARD 214
You know I will, dude.

YELLOW GUARD BETA
Be advised, I'm en route.

TREW
Hey, boys. Are you ready for the race next week?

MASON
Yeah, we are, Trew. We won the race last night, too.

SAMMY
[walkie talkie]
This is Sammy. Jake, Mason, I need you guys to go back to my old house. There's something that's been hiding there for a long time, and I need it back. Good luck.

JAKE
We'll do our best...

SAMMY
[walkie talkie]
You're looking for an old seed... You got it! Thanks, guys. I need you to bring it out to the old forest so my clone can plant it.

JAKE
Hey, Carson, Becker. We need you guys to give us some water for this plant seed, please.

CARSON
No problem, Jake. We can give you guys some water.

MASON
Thanks, Carson. I think this might be a good start to
our friendship.

BECKER
You know, Mason, I was just thinking the same thing.

CARSON
The plant seed is good to go. Bring it to Sammy now.

JAKE
We heard you needed this plant seed, Sammy.

SAMMY 2
Yes, I do need it. Thank you. Now it's time to do my
own mission... In my head, of course.

MASON
Jake, we've got company...

SAMMY 2
Protect me and the seed, boys.

JAKE
You got it, Sammy.

KIG
Hello, boys. Is it okay if I help out, too?

JAKE
Sure, Kig. You can help out.

KIG
Boom, baby! One Metal Creature, fried... Now that's
what I call blowing someone's mind... Nice work, boys.

We got them all. I'll see you later.

MASON
Okay, Kig. We'll see you later.

SAMMY 2
Thank you, boys. I've completed my mission with the
seed.

JAKE
Anytime, Sammy. Let's go, Mason.

HADEN
It's Brother Jake, and his little friend Mason. It's good
to see you guys again.

JAKE
It's good to see you again, Haden.

MASON
I'm not really happy to see him again.

HADEN
It's okay, I'm sure Jake wants to help me out. I need
you guys to free a couple of my friends and send them
back to The Hole.

JAKE
Sure, Haden. We can do that for you.

GUARD 999
I got a bet on the next City races.

GUARD 40
Dryan is my boy. He always wins.

HADEN
I thank you guys again. I recall Dim needing to see you

guys. Until next time.

MASON
Hey there, Dim. How's everything going here?

DIM
I've got good news and bad news. The good news is
that we've got enough power to keep the shields up.
The City is safe for now, I just don't know for how long.

JAKE
And the bad news?

DIM
Do you recall anything about Metal Creature eggs at
the strip mine?

JAKE
I did see a crane moving around what looked like eggs
the last time we were there.

DIM
I thought so. I need you guys to go there and destroy
that crane machine. Now.

JAKE
You got it, Dim.

MASON
Whoa! This place is a little cool, Jake.

JAKE
Yeah, it is. We need to keep moving, buddy. You can
stay safe in my underwear again.

MASON
Okay, Jake.

DIM
Thank you, guys. You've really helped out a lot.

CARCOSA CADEN
Hey, Jake. Mason. It's good to see you guys again.

MASON
Hey, Caden. How's the kid doing?

CARCOSA CADEN
He is doing well. He's resting at my place for now.

JAKE
I'm glad to hear he's doing well... Anyways, Mason, we
should go see Trew again.

KIG
Actually, Trew's been napping for a while. But I think I
know what he'd want you to do.

JAKE
What's that, Kig?

KIG
I think he'd want you boys to go back down into the
sewers and destroy that statue.

MASON
Wait, we have to destroy that statue now, Kig?

KIG
Yes. That might be the last thing Trew will need from
you boys... Oh, and Jake, there are some friends
waiting for you in the sewers.

GAGE
Here come Jake and Mason. It's about time you guys
showed up. Kig told us that you'll protect us when we
get to the statue. I've got everything we need. Just shut

your mouths and keep moving...

ALEXX
Do we have to, Gage?

GAGE
Yes, Alexx, we have to. We go down... This way... Shut
up, you dorks... Metal Creatures up ahead! They're
climbing the walls... Alright, Rob, blow a hole for us...

ALEXX
Geez, Rob, what did you put in those bombs?

GAGE
Your big mouth. Now shut up and keep moving...
We've got company! Jake, get those guys behind us...

ALEXX
Jake is my hero.

GAGE
Shut up, Alexx.

ROB
I think we should go back. Before we all get hurt.

GAGE
How about you guys move your butts, before I move
them for you... Maybe you can be leader next time,
Rob, and see how easy it is... No, Alexx, we're not
almost there. We still have a long way to go. Now shut
up before I kick your butt... Take care of this other
blocked path, Rob...

ALEXX
Maybe we should keep moving now...

GAGE
One more word, Alexx, and I'll beat the crap out of
you... Here we are. Time to blow up that statue.

JAKE
Thanks for the help, guys. We'll let Trew know the
statue is taken care of.

***

EMMA
I've been working on the car that we used to go through
the portal.

JAKE
Nice one, Emma. Now we can go home.

EMMA
Sorry, Jake. We need a final piece to finish it up.

SAMMY
And what's that?

BRYAN
I believe this is the piece that she's talking about,
Sammy.

SAMMY
Bryan? Is that you?

BRYAN
Yes, it is. How have you guys been?

JAKE
We're doing good, Bryan. Where have you been?

BRYAN
My goodness, Jake! You can talk now!

MASON
Baron Hax gave our friend here some new Powers.

EMMA
Oh, Jake! I almost forgot! You need to get ready for the
next race. It's almost time.

JAKE
Don't worry, Emma. I've been ready.

MASON
Jake, is it okay if I stay here with Emma?

JAKE
Sure, Mason.

MASON
And go easy on Dryan, Jake.

JAKE
I'll do my best, buddy.

EMMA
Good luck out there, Jake.

YELLOW GUARD ALPHA
I might be a little late to the race. I'll see you later.

GUARD 590
Okay. We'll see you later, dude.

DRYAN
Hey, Jake. Good luck out there.

JAKE
Thanks, Dryan. Let's do this.

BARON HAX
Welcome, everyone, to the third race. In lane three we
have my new friend, Jake. And in the fourth lane is
Dryan, who is also my friend. Wait until the green
lights, and... Go!

MASON
Go Jake! Go Dryan!

BARON HAX
And we have a winner! Jake came in first place,

followed by Dryan! Jake, please join me at the palace later.

JAKE
Umm, thanks, Baron.

BARON HAX
But be careful. There's war going on between my guards right now.

GUARD 309
There they are! Get them!

BARON HAX
Darn it, they're already here.

JAKE
Dryan, no!

DRYAN
I'm okay, Jake. Go on without me, I'll try to hold them off here. Get your little friend and go.

JAKE
Okay, Dryan. Thanks for the help.

DRYAN
Anytime, Jake. I'll always be your friend.

GUARD 309
After him!

GUARD 509
Hello, you little dorks. You guys are after our new friends?

GUARD 309
Yes, now get out of our way.

GUARD 509
Sorry, but Baron Hax's orders. We protect our friends.

GUARD 309
Then you leave us no choice. Guys, they're asking for it!
Take care of the guards, then the boys!

GILBERT
Hello there, Jake and Mason. I'm glad that I finally get
to meet you.

JAKE
Do we know you?

GILBERT
No, but you will. I'm Gilbert, William's boss. And if you
want to stop me, you'll have to find me in the caves at
the top of the mountains.

JAKE
Just wait. We'll be there soon, Gilbert.

TAMMY
Jake, Mason, I'm sorry, but I need you to put your
hands up.

JAKE
Oh good, you're back to being mean to us.

TAMMY
I'm sorry, but I don't think you can be with us
anymore.

JAKE
Wait, Tammy! We're on your side!

TAMMY
I know, Jake. Dim, get in here.

DIM
What? What? Can't you see I'm kind of busy here,
Tammy?

TAMMY
How long until the bomb goes off?

DIM
Man, let's see, after some quick calculations... It's
gonna be hard to tell... Maybe... An hour?

TAMMY
An hour.

DIM
Yes, Tammy. An hour before the bomb goes off. Now if
you don't mind, I'm gonna go throw up. Bye bye.

JAKE
Tammy, we need to get to the caves to stop Gilbert. You
know we can do it, but we have to be fast.

TAMMY
Stopping Gilbert and his bomb is going to be hard,
but... Okay. You can try. Good luck, guys.

JAKE
Thanks, Tammy.

YELLOW GUARD GAMMA
Searching for suspects...

GILBERT
Well well well, I'm glad you made it.

JAKE
Yeah, I'm looking forward to stopping you, Gilbert.
And your friend William, too.

GILBERT
Oh, really? Because when I'm done with you, William
and I will get back to Baron Hax and make him pay.

JAKE
I think you may need some help with your own dreams
there.

GILBERT
I know everything about you and your no-good friends.
I know every move you've made since coming to LA. I'll
take care of them all. But first, you and that boy hiding
in your underwear.

JAKE
I don't think so, Gilbert.

GILBERT
Then it's war, huh? Fine. I'll take you down now.

JAKE
No! My sword!

GILBERT
Yes! Now you have nothing to fight me with, and you're
all alone... Hey, what the heck?

TREW
They're not alone, Gilbert, but you are.

JAKE & MASON
Trew!

GILBERT
Fine, I'll take you down first, you butthead.

TREW
Bring it.

JAKE
Trew, no!

GILBERT
Your friend Trew has gone bye bye.

TREW
I may be down, but I'm not out.

GILBERT
What? No!

MASON
That's what you get for stabbing our friend, Gilbert.

TREW
Boys, come here. You still have that ruby key, right? I
need you to help Kig open its door.

JAKE
Okay, Trew. We will help Kig out.

GILBERT
I can't let you guys leave.

JAKE
Too late, we're leaving now.

TAMMY
Over here, guys. And fast.

MASON
Jake, look at that explosion!

JAKE
Goodbye, Trew. We'll miss you.

TAMMY
I'll find my dad, you guys go find Kig.

HESSY
Hey, guys! I was just looking at this cool game that
Trew left out, but I'm not sure if it works...

MASON
Well, whatever it is, Trew won't be needing it
anymore... Man, where's Kig when you need him?

HESSY
Kig! I think Trew sent him to do another mission. I
think he said something about a secret door? I'm not
sure...

JAKE
Let's go.

HESSY
Be careful out there, guys. I'll bring this thing to
Emma.

MASON
I'll be back, Hessy, then we can play some games
together! Jake... Where did all these Metal Creatures
come from? I'm just going to hide in your underwear
until this war is over.

DIM
Ahhh! Guys, help! The shields are down, and the Metal
Creatures are in the City!

JAKE
Just wait here, we'll take care of it.

YELLOW GUARD BETA
Shoot that thing! Shoot it!

GUARD 2319
Move in!

GUARD 116
Fire! Fire!

YELLOW GUARD ALPHA
Go! Go!

JAKE
Hey there, tough guy.

KIG
Get your little butts over here and start fighting. Man, I love this job. I'll have to thank Trew for this job next time I see him, it's been a lot of fun watching you guys get the ruby key and finding the secret door...

JAKE
Trew's dead, Kig.

KIG
What? Why? What happened to him, Jake?

JAKE
Trew tried to help us against Gilbert and he got stabbed.

KIG
Oh man, I wanted to be there with you boys. I'm sorry, I didn't know.

MASON
Then the bomb went off. Now Trew and Gilbert are both gone.

JAKE
Let's get out of here.

KIG
If I can't shoot it, it's someone else's problem... Move
your butts! Shooting it will only make it mad... Run!
Faster!

JAKE
Let's go, Kig. We're almost to the palace elevator.

KIG
It looks like we finally lost him. That was some great
teamwork back there. Now let's take this fight to
William. He'll never see it coming! And after that, we
can do something fun. Us guys, saving the world, side
by side, we're...

JAKE & MASON
Kig! No!

KIG
Ahhhhh!

MASON
So... What's plan B?

***

EMMA
The car is finished, but my dad has figured out that the portal is in the Metal Creatures' nest.

HADEN
I think I can help with that. My friends and I built a balloon that can get you right to that nest.

MASON
Haden, you're officially awesome now.

JAKE
Okay, you guys get the car to the nest using the balloon. We'll meet you there.

MASON
Oh man, I wanted to go on the balloon ride with Emma, Jake.

JAKE
Don't worry, Mason. You get to ride in my underwear again.

MASON
Yes, I've been very lucky today.

HADEN
I think we're ready now. Time to go to the nest... Oh, here come the Metal dorks...

JAKE
Don't worry, Haden. I'll deal with them

DIM
Jake, I want you guys to know that I'm gonna be staying here. I think it's pretty safe. Have fun getting back to your home, I'll miss you.

JAKE
Caden, what's going on?

CARCOSA CADEN
It's okay, Jake. Baron Hax and I are just looking for
William now. We think he's somewhere down here, but
it's dark so we can't be sure. We could definitely use
your help.

JAKE
We'll look for William.

WILLIAM
Well well well, look who we have here. If it isn't Jake,
Mason, Baron Hax, and Mr. Carcosa. I've been waiting
for you. And what's with all the back-up, Hax? Don't
you trust me?

BARON HAX
Just shut up, William. We're here to stop you.

WILLIAM
Oh, really? It'd be so much easier if you all stood down
and passed over the kid and the key.

BARON HAX
We will never let you hurt the kid.

WILLIAM
Well then, I'm afraid this is how it ends for you, Baron
Hax. And you too, Caden.

BARON HAX
Charge!

WILLIAM
Hahaha, now I can resume my search in peace. Catch
you boys later. In my nest.

BARON HAX
Jake, please protect this City for me. I've always looked to you as a son. And please tell Tammy I'm sorry... About everything.

CARCOSA CADEN
Jake, protect the kid. Win this war.

JAKE
You did your best, and we will, too.

***

TAMMY
This is not good. The Metal Creatures are still on the move. We need a way to stop them, and fast.

ZORN
[walkie talkie]
Jake, get to the nest. If you can defeat William, you'll take care of the Metal Creatures, too.

MASON
Whoa. This place is a little scary, Jake.

TAMMY
This is it, Jake. You just have to put the key in that slot. Once you guys are in the nest, we'll be able to help you out.

MASON
Okay, Jake. Let's hope this works.

JAKE
Let's go in.

MASON
Wait, what? You mean go in there?

JAKE
Yeah... Why?

MASON
Uh, nothing. I just think I might get scared in there.

WILLIAM
You finally decided to join us. Now I can use the key to take over the City.

MASON
Hey, William, I won't let you take over LA. I love it

here. I won't let you get away with this.

WILLIAM
Oh, Mason, still living in your dreams, I see. I will take over LA, and I will do it with this kid. You see him, Jake? He's you, when you were six years old. If you want him back, you'll have to take him from me.

JAKE
I thought you'd never ask.

WILLIAM
Bring it on.

JAKE
No, my sword!

WILLIAM
What's the matter, Jake? Can't fight without your sword? Hey... What the...

BRYAN
They're not alone, William. I'm here to help them.

SAMMY
Me, too.

SAMMY 2
Don't forget the rest of us.

JAKE & MASON
Bryan! Sammy! Emma! Tammy! Haden! Zorn!

WILLIAM
Oh, come on. Must you guys always interrupt me when I'm about to deal the finishing blow?

ZORN
You know we will. Stand down.

TAMMY
Don't make this hard for you.

WILLIAM
Hey, what the heck?

JAKE
Good, while he was distracted, we got him.

EMMA
Yes! We stopped William! Now we just need to go
home...

JAKE
No, Emma. We're already home.

SAMMY
What do you mean, Jake?

JAKE
I mean Los Angeles is our home now. I promised
Mason we can live here forever.

SAMMY
That's nice of you, Jake. But what do we do with the
kid?

JAKE
The kid is me. I think the other Sammy should watch
over him.

SAMMY 2
Wait, you don't mean... Oh, okay. I will do it for you
guys. I'll go back to Miami with him. Take care of
yourselves here.

JAKE
Don't worry, Sammy. We will.

SAMMY 2
Goodbye, everyone. I'll miss you all.

BRYAN
Sammy, over here.

SAMMY
Bryan, are you okay?

BRYAN
It's time for me to go, too.

SAMMY
Don't worry, Bryan. We will take care of everything for
you, my old friend.

***

HADEN
Is everything okay now, Tammy?

TAMMY
Yes, thank you, Captain Haden. Come on, Zorn. We're
gonna be late for the party at Mason's new place.

ZORN
Let's go.

MASON
Welcome to my new place!

CARSON
Wow, this place is awesome, Mason!

BECKER
And you sure know how to throw a party.

MASON
Thanks, guys. That means a lot to me.

JAKE
I still can't believe that little boy was me. Good times.

EMMA
You really miss him, don't you, Jake? But on the bright
side, at least that little boy will grow up to be a great
hero someday... Who's that over there?

CORBIN
I'm Corbin.

MASON
Ah! A Metal Creature.

JAKE
Kig!

MASON
Kig? I knew that.

JAKE
You're okay!

KIG
You didn't think I'd miss the biggest party ever, did
you?

MASON
It's good to see that you're still alive, Kig.

HADEN
Your friend Mason is a very nice kid, Jake.

JAKE
Thanks, Haden. We're a great team.

SAMMY
Jake, my boy, the future awaits.

THE ADVENTURES OF JAKE AND MASON

3

VENDER
By the laws of Los Angeles and its people, you are
banished from LA for life. You are in LA, and now you
must leave.

TAMMY
This isn't cool, Vender. We will destroy what you've
done.

VENDER
Your friendship was getting tiresome. If you had just
followed my orders and stayed away from him, none of
this would have happened. Now set him free.

CARSON
Stop right there, Vender. I'm tired of your mouth
flapping about my friend Jake, and now I have
something to say. Not everyone hates him for what he
did. Not his friends.

CORBIN
If you set him free, it better be to let him come back to
LA with us.

BECKER
I agree with these guys, Vender. Let him be a hero in
LA.

MASON
Yeah, we'll stop you, Vender.

VENDER
Oh, is that so?

CARSON
If you banish Jake, you'll have to banish us, too.

BECKER
We stay together. As friends.

MASON
We'll find a way, Vender. You'll never walk again!

JAKE
Okay, Mason. We get the idea.

TAMMY
I'm sorry, Jake. A lot of the people are ticked at you.
There's nothing I could have done.

JAKE
I know, Tammy. You did your best to help us out back
there.

TAMMY
Hold onto these ear mics so we can stay in contact. We
will be back to find you.

VENDER
Let this new Power take over!

BECKER
Man, this stinks so bad, Carson.

CARSON
It's okay, Becker. We'll find a way back to LA soon.
We'll have to stay here in Vegas for a while.

CORBIN
I heard that Las Vegas is no place for kids, you guys.
And we are kids, you know.

CARSON
I know that, Corbin. Just don't worry about it. It won't
be for long.

MASON
Whatever you're up to, Carson, I want in.

JAKE
Come on, guys. Let's get a move on.

MASON
You got it, Jake.

BECKER
This is all Vender's fault, Carson.

CARSON
I know, Becker. We just need to make the best of it for now.

MASON
I can't believe that the City hates us. We saved their lives!

ZORN
[walkie talkie]
Jake, more bad news: the Metal Creatures are back, with their new friends the Alloid Animals. My men are getting their butts kicked trying to figure out who their new leader is.

SAMMY
Rhinos, lions, tigers, cats, dogs...

JAKE
Wait a minute. Didn't we already destroy William, Sammy?

SAMMY
I'm not sure who their leader is, Jake. The war has only just begun.

TAMMY
We're going to try to stop them, Jake. The people are blaming you for the attack

JAKE
Okay, guys. I think we need to take a little break.

SAMMY
Come in, Zorn.

ZORN
This is bad, Sammy. The Metal Creatures and the Alloid Animals are working together to find something here in the City. And I think that they have brought some of their old friends, too. They might be really bad as well.

TAMMY.
There's also a meeting at city hall today. We think it's about Jake. Something about a bomb?

JAKE
Do you believe that, Sammy?

SAMMY
This isn't the time, Jake. Metal Creatures and Alloid Animals are destroying the City, and I have no idea what to do.

MASON
Nooooo! We're falling!

ZORN
Over here, guys.

SAMMY
This is not good at all.

CAPTAIN HUNTER
Hello, new guys. What brings you to Las Vegas?

JAKE
We were sent here by Vender. He's banished us from
Los Angeles for life.

CAPTAIN HUNTER
Really? For life, huh? Well, maybe you guys can stay
with us.

JAKE
Wait, you want us to stay in Las Vegas with you?

CAPTAIN HUNTER
Sure, just until I can get you back into LA.

JAKE
Okay, we can stay for a while. I'm Jake, and this is my
best friend Mason. This is Carson and his friend
Becker. And that's Corbin. He's nice to everyone, so try
to be nice to him.

CAPTAIN HUNTER
Don't worry, I'll be nice to everyone. My name's
Captain Hunter. I'm a cop. Let's get going, there's a
lightning storm coming in.

JAKE
Okay. Lead the way, Captain Hunter.

MASON
Are you sure about this, Jake?

JAKE
Yeah, I think we can stay with Captain Hunter for a
while, Mason.

MASON
Okay. I was just asking.

CAPTAIN HUNTER
Here we are, guys. You can stay here at the police
station until I find you a hotel.

JAKE
Wow. Thanks, Captain Hunter. This police station is
pretty cool from the outside.

CARSON
Are all these guys here your friends, Captain Hunter?

CAPTAIN HUNTER
Yes, these guys are my friends. And there's a training
place over there for you to use.

MASON
Umm, Captain Hunter? Jake and I are trying to
become heroes, and are kind of trying to save the
world. Maybe we should do the training thing. Can we?
Please?

CAPTAIN HUNTER
Yeah, sure, Mason. Go on ahead and use it.

JAKE
Okay. Come on, Mason. Let's do some training, buddy.

MASON
Can I be in your underwear for it, Jake?

JAKE
Sure, you can be in my underwear for it.

MASON
Thanks, Jake.

JAKE
No problem, Mason.

BECKER
We'll be watching you guys!

CAPTAIN HUNTER
Yeah, there is a TV so you guys can watch them do their
training. And Jake, be warned: there'll be some
fighting in there!

JAKE
You got it, Captain.

BECKER
Jake is doing good so far, Carson.

CARSON
I know, Becker. I think Jake and Mason are going to be
awesome heroes someday.

BECKER
I have to agree with you there, buddy.

CORBIN
I don't get it, guys.

CARSON
What's wrong, Corbin?

CORBIN
How can Mason fit in Jake's underwear like that? I
mean, look at Mason. He's in Jake's underwear almost
like a little joey kangaroo.

BECKER
Come on, Corbin. He likes to be in Jake's underwear a
lot. He wants to wear diapers again, too. Just like you,
remember?

CORBIN
Yeah, I guess you're right, Becker. I will give him a
chance.

JAKE
Yes! We did it, Mason.

MASON
Oh yeah, we are back!

CAPTAIN HUNTER
You guys were great in there. Think you guys can stand
up to a fight now?

JAKE
Yeah, I think I can really fight.

CAPTAIN HUNTER
Awesome. Head back in there and take down those ten
guys. Then you'll be free to wander around Vegas.

JAKE
You got it, Captain Hunter.

MASON
Okay, Jake. Good luck!

JAKE
Hey, thanks, buddy. I'll do my best. I think I might
even use my new Power, too.

MASON
Just be careful, Jake.

JAKE
Don't worry, Mason, I will.

CAPTAIN HUNTER
Is something wrong, Jake?

BECKER
Umm, Captain Hunter, our friend Jake has a new
Power inside him now.

MASON
Yeah, and he uses it when he's mad. So don't make him
mad, Captain.

CAPTAIN HUNTER
Oh no, that's not good. Jake's got the new Power inside
him? I'll be sure not to make him mad. You'll be free to
go once he's done.

CARSON
Good. Thanks, Captain Hunter.

CAPTAIN HUNTER
No problem, Carson. I'll try to find you guys a hotel to
stay at soon.

LIEUTENANT ORION
That was some good fighting you did in there, dude. I
was really impressed with how you fought all those
dudes in there.

JAKE
Are you talking to me?

MASON
Yeah, are you talking to him, dude?

LIEUTENANT ORION
No, I was talking to myself... Yes, I was talking to you!
The new guys here in Las Vegas! I can't believe you're
here after everything that's happened to you guys

today.

JAKE
How do you know about all that?

LIEUTENANT ORION
I can tell a lot about a guy just by looking at him. My name's Orion, but my friends call me Lieutenant. Captain Hunter over there has been my best friend since fifth grade.

BECKER
And let me guess, you're a cop, too?

LIEUTENANT ORION
Yes, I'm a new guy on the force. If you need any help, just ask. But first, I need to ask a favor of you dudes.

CARSON
Whatever you need, Lieutenant Orion. My name is Carson. These are my friends Jake and Mason, and this is my friend Becker. And this is Corbin, our nice friend. Be nice to him.

LIEUTENANT ORION
Don't worry, I'll be nice to Corbin. Now, I need you to take down these guys in red. There are four of them, and they're all over the City. Split up and get them.

JAKE
Don't worry, Lieutenant Orion. You can count on us.

BECKER
Carson and I will go that way.

CORBIN
I'll go after that guy over there.

JAKE
And we'll go after those two guys.

BECKER
Good luck, guys.

MASON
Thanks, Becker. You guys need some luck, too.

JAKE
Okay, Mason, time to be quiet now.

BECKER
Wow! Nice shot, Carson.

CARSON
Thanks, Becker. My practice is paying off.

BECKER
I know, buddy. I'm always watching your practices,
remember?

CARSON
I think we should wait here until the other guys are
done with their targets.

BECKER
That's a good plan, Carson. I'm down with it.

CORBIN
Got mine.

JAKE
Yes! That's one of ours down. Only one more to go...
And done.

CORBIN
Nice one, Jake. You got your two guys.

JAKE
Hey, thanks. I always try my best destroying bad guys...
Alright, Mason, you can talk now.

MASON
Okay, thanks, Jake.

LIEUTENANT ORION
Nice work, boys. I think we can definitely help each
other out. See you around.

CARSON
Hey, check out those ladies over there. They seem to
working on something... Hey, are you ladies okay?

MANDY
It's nothing important.

CARSON
Sorry. We're new in town, and trying to get back to LA.
We thought we could help out while we're waiting.

MANDY
Oh, I'm sorry. I'm Mandy, we work with people who
are new here. I guess we could use your help.

JAKE
We can try.

MASON
Be careful, Jake. I'll be right here next to Carson.

MANDY
Wow, you did that faster than I ever could.

JAKE
I always try my best.

MANDY
You can stick around, if you want.

CORBIN
Umm, sorry to interrupt, Mandy, but we need to go
now.

BECKER
Uh, guys... I think that thing is moving.

CARSON
Why is it moving?

MANDY
I'm not sure. What did you do?

JAKE
I was doing what you told me to do.

MASON
Okay, I'm done now.

CORBIN
Whoa, that was crazy.

BECKER
I agree, Corbin, that thing was moving crazy fast.

CORBIN
What was that, Mason?

MASON
I'm not sure, Corbin. But I think we'll find out soon.

MANDY
I don't know what that was all about, but my crew and I
have to go. Please get away while you can. We'll see you
soon.

JAKE
Okay. See you around, Mandy.

MASON
I think we should go, Jake.

JAKE
Let's get a move on, guys.

***

LIEUTENANT ORION
Look at that, it's the new guys. It's good to see you guys
again. How are you dudes doing?

CARSON
We're fine, Lieutenant. We just made some new
friends.

LIEUTENANT ORION
That's cool, Carson. I have something to ask you guys.

BECKER
Whatever it is, Lieutenant Orion, I'm sure we can do it.

LIEUTENANT ORION
Actually, Becker, this is for Jake... I need him to be in a
race, if he wants.

JAKE
What kind of race am I gonna be in?

LIEUTENANT ORION
It's just a race, Jake. A normal race that everyone does.
Three laps. I'll be in it, too.

JAKE
Really? Okay, Lieutenant Orion. I'll be in the race.

BECKER
Good luck, Jake.

JAKE
Thanks, Becker. I will do my best in the race, guys.

LIEUTENANT ORION
Ready... Set... Go!

JAKE
Yes, I won the race.

LIEUTENANT ORION
Well, I have to say you were awesome, Jake. You really gave it to me. First time I ever lost a race. I'll see you dudes later.

JAKE
Okay, Lieutenant Orion. We'll see you later.

CAPTAIN HUNTER
Awesome race, Jake. I heard that was Lieutenant Orion's doing.

JAKE
Yeah. He asked me to race, and I won.

CAPTAIN HUNTER
You seem happy about winning the race.

MASON
Yeah, Jake always gets happy winning races, Captain Hunter. Be prepared, I'll be doing a victory dance for him!

BECKER
Yeah, best get prepared. He's gonna be doing a victory dance!

CARSON
Please stop it, Becker. We get it.

BECKER
Sorry, Carson. I'll shut up now.

CAPTAIN HUNTER
I have to go, guys. I'll see you around.

MASON
See you around, Captain Hunter.

BECKER
Hey, Carson, look: it's Mandy again.

CARSON
Yeah, you're right, Becker. Hello, Mandy! How are you
doing today?

MANDY
I'm doing fine, Carson. You guys remember my friends.

BECKER
Yeah, we remember your friends, Mandy. It's good to
see you again

LIZ
Hey, that kid has a talking animal on his shoulder!

ASHLEY
Yeah! Why does he have that, Mandy?

MANDY
It's okay, girls. He's Carson's good friend. What's your
name?

BECKER
Ladies, my name is Becker. Sorry if I frightened you. I
used to be a human, but now I am a tiger—the most
awesome animal in the world.

MANDY
It's nice to meet you, Becker. These are my friends Liz
and Ashley. Now we are all introduced.

JAKE
It's nice to meet your friends, Mandy. I hope we can all

be friends.

LIZ
Yeah, I think we can be friends with you guys.

ASHLEY
I will try my best not to yell at you.

MASON
Well, we're trying to become heroes, Ashley. You'll
probably yell at us a lot.

ASHLEY
Wait, did I say yell? I meant scream at you guys.

LIZ
That's better, Ashley.

ASHLEY
Thanks, Liz.

BECKER
I think we should go now, Carson.

CARSON
Okay, Becker. It was nice to meet you, girls.

MANDY
Come on, girls. Let's go.

CORBIN
Hey, Becker, how old are you?

BECKER
I'm glad you asked, Corbin. I'm 19. I'm an adult now!

JAKE
I think we should go and see Captain Hunter again.

Let's go.

CORBIN
Lead the way, Jake.

CAPTAIN HUNTER
I'm glad you could make it. Jake, this is my friend
Ralph. We call him Lieutenant Ralph. I need you to
have a fun fight with him.

JAKE
I'll do my best, sir.

LIEUTENANT RALPH
Hello, everyone. My name is Lieutenant Ralph. I will
be having a fun fight with Jake.

JAKE
Yeah, I'm looking forward to it.

LIEUTENANT RALPH
Awesome. Let's go in, Jake.

JAKE
Okay. Just let me put Mason in my underwear first.

LIEUTENANT RALPH
Sure, Jake. I'll wait for you in there.

JAKE
You got it, Lieutenant Ralph.

CORBIN
Good luck, Jake.

LIEUTENANT RALPH
Wow, you destroyed me, Jake.

BECKER
I can't believe that you just beat Lieutenant Ralph in that fun fight, Jake.

MASON
I was thinking we should have a fun fight, too, Becker.

BECKER
I was just thinking the same thing.

CAPTAIN HUNTER
Okay, guys, stop it. If I wanted you two to fun fight, I would've asked for it... Good work, Jake. Keep it up and you'll be back to LA in no time.

JAKE
Cool. Thanks, Captain Hunter. We'll be walking around again.

LIEUTENANT ORION
Hey, guys. I have a job for Jake and Mason, if you don't mind.

JAKE
What is it, Lieutenant Orion? I think we can do it.

LIEUTENANT ORION
You guys have heard of Metal Creatures, yeah?

JAKE
Yeah...

LIEUTENANT ORION
Well, they have friends now. Alloid Animals.

MASON
And what kinds of Alloid Animals are there, Lieutenant?

LIEUTENANT ORION
Rhinos, lions, bears. I need you to go out and destroy some. Keep an eye out, one might have a special device...

***

DRYAN
[walkie talkie]
Jake, Mason, are you guys out there? It's me, Dryan.
I'm still alive. If you get this message, know that I'm
still with you, and I want to help you get back to LA.

JAKE
I'm not so sure about that voice, Mason.

MASON
Yeah, it almost sounded like someone we've met here
in Las Vegas.

BECKER
How did it go, guys?

JAKE
It was cool, Becker. We destroyed them fast as lighting.

BECKER
Carson, look, it's Mandy.

MANDY
Hey, it's good to see you again. How are you guys?

CARSON
We're good, Mandy. We were just watching Jake fight
some Alloid Animals.

MANDY
Wow, that's really cool. We need to get going, but we'll
see you again soon.

JAKE
I think Lieutenant Orion needs us again.

CARSON
Okay, Jake. Let's go see Lieutenant Orion.

LIEUTENANT ORION
Captain Hunter has a job for us. Just listen to me and you'll be okay.

MASON
You got it, Lieutenant Orion.

CAPTAIN HUNTER
How's it going, guys?

LIEUTENANT ORION
It's going good, sir. Just talking to Jake and his friends about our mission.

CAPTAIN HUNTER
I know you guys are still new around here, but Jake, didn't your father ever teach you to make your own choices?

JAKE
I don't think I ever actually met my father, Captain Hunter.

CAPTAIN HUNTER
I'm sorry to hear that, Jake. But I hope you understand me. I want you to start making your own choices.

JAKE
Yes, I understand.

CAPTAIN HUNTER
I was hoping you'd say that. Now go out with Lieutenant Orion. I need you guys to save three giant kangaroos. Just like you've seen on TV.

JAKE
No problem, Captain Hunter. Carson is good with animals.

CARSON
Yeah, I am good with this. I'll do fine with Becker at my
side.

CORBIN
Remember, he wants us to work together with
Lieutenant Orion.

CARSON
I know, Corbin. You know what I mean, buddy.

BECKER
And look at Jake, Corbin. He has Mason in his
underwear… He's kind of like a kangaroo himself.

CARSON
We get it, Becker.

BECKER
Sorry, Carson.

CARSON
It's okay.

LIEUTENANT ORION
Okay, let's get a move on now.

JAKE
Okay, Lieutenant Orion. You can lead the way this
time.

LIEUTENANT ORION
Thanks, Jake. I'll make sure these guys do okay,
Captain Hunter.

CAPTAIN HUNTER
I know, Lieutenant Orion. I know you will do your best.

LIEUTENANT ORION
And I will be coming back with them in my cool, sweet ride, sir.

CAPTAIN HUNTER
Please leave, Lieutenant.

LIEUTENANT ORION
You got it, Captain.

BECKER
You know, Carson, Las Vegas has been pretty good to you so far. You've even met three girls.

CARSON
Becker, can you please not go there? I don't want to talk about it.

BECKER
You got it, buddy. I'm sorry.

CARSON
It's okay, Becker. I forgive you.

LIEUTENANT ORION
Here we are, guys. And there are the kangaroos that Captain Hunter was talking about.

CORBIN
Wait, Lieutenant Orion. What kind of kangaroos are they? Are they red kangaroos, or common kangaroos, or...

LIEUTENANT ORION
Just normal kangaroos, Corbin. You, Carson, and Mason will be the ones in their pouches. And everyone can pet them. They are very friendly.

MASON
Awesome! I get to ride in a kangaroo pouch for my first time. I'll be a cool kid.

LIEUTENANT ORION
Once you boys are in the pouches, I have leashes for each of their necks.

CARSON
You got it, Lieutenant Orion. I think Mason should go first. He's really good with being in Jake's underwear.

MASON
Yeah, I think I can go first. Carson can go after me.

LIEUTENANT ORION
Okay, Mason. You can go first.

MASON
I'm right behind you.

JAKE
Good luck, Mason.

MASON
Thanks, Jake. I'll do my best.

LIEUTENANT ORION
Okay, Mason. You're in the kangaroo's pouch now, buddy.

MASON
Cool.

LIEUTENANT ORION
Now that I've got its leash on, I can bring it back to the pen. Be careful, Mason. You might get sick with the hopping.

MASON
I'll try not to.

LIEUTENANT ORION
Okay, Mason, I'm afraid you need to come out now.

MASON
Oh man, that stinks. I want to stay in this pouch for a
while, Lieutenant Orion.

LIEUTENANT ORION
I'm sorry, Mason. You'll have to talk to Jake about that.

MASON
Okay, Lieutenant Orion. I'll talk to Jake about having a
kangaroo for a pet.

LIEUTENANT ORION
Okay, Carson. It's your turn.

CARSON
Alright. This will be my first time, too.

LIEUTENANT ORION
Glad I can make you happy.

CARSON
Wow. So this is what it feels like to be in a kangaroo
pouch.

LIEUTENANT ORION
You have to come out now, Carson.

CARSON
I was really enjoying myself. I'll have to do it again
someday.

LIEUTENANT ORION
Maybe when you guys come back to Vegas, the captain
can borrow these kangaroos for you.

CARSON
It's a deal, Lieutenant Orion.

LIEUTENANT ORION
Okay, Carson. Let's go see Becker again, buddy.

CARSON
I'll beat you there.

LIEUTENANT ORION
Okay, Corbin. Your turn.

CORBIN
I'm ready.

LIEUTENANT ORION
Okay, come here. I'll carry you there.

CORBIN
Thanks, Lieutenant.

LIEUTENANT ORION
Okay, guys. Let's head back now.

JAKE
Okay, Lieutenant Orion. Let's head back, guys.

MASON
Lead the way, Jake.

LIEUTENANT ORION
Hang on there, guys. I've got a really sweet ride we can
all go back in.

BECKER
What kind of sweet ride are you talking about,
Lieutenant Orion?

LIEUTENANT ORION
This cool van over here. It fits, like, six people in it.

JAKE
We know how many people fit in vans, Lieutenant. I
call shotgun.

MASON
I'm gonna sit right behind you, Jake.

CARSON
I'm gonna sit right behind Lieutenant Orion.

CORBIN
I'm going to sit behind Carson.

BECKER
I'm just going to sit on your lap, Carson.

LIEUTENANT ORION
This is my cool van, and it is mine.

***

MASON
Hey, Jake. I think there's someone spying on us. Let's
check it out.

JAKE
Okay, Mason. I'll check it out... Kig?

KIG
Jake? Mason?

MASON
Kig!

KIG
It's good to see you guys again!

JAKE
What are you doing here, Kig?

KIG
I'm here to help you guys in your missions. But first...
Let's do this, Jake.

JAKE
Whoa! Hang on, Kig. I don't want to fight you.

KIG
It's okay, Jake. It's just a fun fight.

CAPTAIN HUNTER
You'd better not hurt my friend.

KIG
Don't worry, sir, I won't. Jake and I are friends, too.
We need to speak in your office.

LIEUTENANT ORION
I'll bring them in, Captain Hunter.

CAPTAIN HUNTER
Okay, Lieutenant. I'll be waiting.

LIEUTENANT ORION
Corbin, Carson, Becker: I need you guys to stay out
here with Mason, okay?

CARSON
Okay, Lieutenant Orion. We will stay out here with
Mason.

MASON
What's going on, Carson?

BECKER
Captain Hunter is talking to Jake and Kig in his office.

MASON
Oh, okay.

CAPTAIN HUNTER
So what did you need to talk to me about?

KIG
We just need to talk about our upcoming mission.

CAPTAIN HUNTER
There are some bad gas machines out there that are
illegal in Las Vegas. I need you to destroy them for me.

KIG
Okay. Come on, Jake. Let's go destroy those illegal gas
machines together... Jake, look out! You got company
heading your way, buddy... Just use your sword to
destroy those Alloid Animals... Good job, Jake. I'm
done with my gas machines. It's up to you now...
Awesome, let's head back to the police station now.

TAMMY
[walkie talkie]
Jake, Mason: this is Tammy. I'm glad Hunter found
you guys. I need you to come find me. We need to talk.

JAKE
Tammy! Kig, I need you to help Captain Hunter watch
Corbin, Becker, and Carson.

CAPTAIN HUNTER
Don't worry, Jake. Kig and I will watch them for you.

JAKE
Come on, Mason. We need to visit an old friend.

MASON
Hey, Tammy! It's so good to see you again, since the
last time we hung out Vender banished us from LA for
life.

JAKE
Tammy... What brings you here?

TAMMY
You know I'm sorry I couldn't help you guys.

JAKE
Vender will pay for what he did. But enough about that.
How are you? How is everyone?

TAMMY
Everyone's fine. Zorn misses you. He might not say it
outright, but he never stops talking about you guys,
and...

JAKE
Look out, Tammy!

MASON
Oh crap, it's those guys again. I hope you and Tammy
can take them on, Jake.

JAKE
Let's do this.

TAMMY
I can't take you guys back to Los Angeles with me, but I
did see an airport on my way here. That could be your
ticket in.

JAKE
Come on, Mason. We need to go back to the police
station and tell the others.

***

JAKE
Captain Hunter, I want to take a plane back to LA. We
need to see our friends again.

CAPTAIN HUNTER
I know how you feel, Jake. I'd like to see my son again.

JAKE
You have a kid, Captain?

CAPTAIN HUNTER
Yes, I did. I mean, I do. He's nineteen, just like you. His
biggest dream was to be ten years old again. I hope
someday I can make his wish come true. If I ever see
him again.

JAKE
And what's your son's name, Captain Hunter?

CAPTAIN HUNTER
His name is Mack.

JAKE
I'll try to find him in LA for you, sir.

CAPTAIN HUNTER
Here you go, Jake. You guys are ready to go back home.

JAKE
Thanks, Captain Hunter. We'll come back and help you
out any time.

CAPTAIN HUNTER
I know you will. Now get going.

***

KIG
Man oh man, I'm happy to be back in LA, guys.

JAKE
Me too, Kig. Come on, guys. Let's go find the others.

BECKER
Lead the way, Jake.

VENDER
Well well well, look who's back in Los Angeles. I thought I banished you dorks.

JAKE
Well, we had some unfinished business.

VENDER
Sorry, Jake, but I'm a bit busy right now. We can take care of this later.

KIG
Oh, no way, Vender. Jake is ready to take you on now, and we're here to help him.

VENDER
Oh really? By working together as friends? Fine, you guys win. But I have friends, too. Have fun with my giant robot. I'd wish you luck, but I don't wish anyone luck.

KIG
Come back here, Vender! We're not finished with you, punk!

BECKER
Kig, wait. There's a robot over there.

KIG
Darn it. We need to destroy that thing before we can
move on... Yes! We did it, Jake. That robot is down and
out.

MASON
Wow, this place reminds me of my room in Miami. And
I never cleaned my room in Miami. True story, guys.

SAMMY
Hey, Jake. Over here.

JAKE
Hey, Sammy, Emma.

MASON
Uh, Sammy. It's really good to see you again. And
Emma, too.

SAMMY
You see, Emma? I told you that Jake would come to us
again. Jake, these shields are blocking you from
coming to this side of the City with us.

JAKE
Wow, I see what you mean, Sammy. We'll find another
way in. Tell the others we'll be there soon.

SAMMY
You know I will, my boy. And listen, Jake: I'm sorry
about what happened with Vender. We'll talk about
how to beat him later.

JAKE
I know, Sammy. We'll see you two again soon. I hope.

KIG
Wow. Okay, guys, we're back in LA. That was easier

than I thought it'd be.

JAKE
It's good to be back. Now we need to find Mason's
place, the restaurant.

MASON
Oh yeah, we need to find my restaurant.

KIG
Don't worry, guys. I found it in the first place, before
we were friends, and I found it again. Plus, I think all
these guys here are on our side.

JAKE
Great, looks like we have an army.

MASON
Thanks, Kig. It feels good to be back... Hess, I'm home!

ZORN
Jake. I never thought I'd see you guys again.

MASON
Zorn, what's with all this stuff?

ZORN
I'm trying to figure out who's behind the Metal
Creatures and the Alloid Animals. It really
complements the décor, huh?

MASON
Oh, yeah...

ZORN
Listen, Jake. I'm sorry I didn't help more when Vender
banished you.

JAKE
I know you guys did what you could. We saw Vender at the airport.

BECKER
But Vender had a big robot in our way, so Jake and Kig teamed up and destroyed it.

CARSON
Okay, enough, Becker. We have enough problems trying to figure out this new leader of the Metal Creatures and the Alloid Animals.

MASON
Don't worry, Carson. We'll figure it out without any trouble.

ZORN
Speaking of trouble, we have robotic soldiers on their way here. Think you can take them, Jake?

JAKE
You know I can, Zorn.

***

DRYAN
[walkie talkie]
Hey, Jake. It's good to see you again, glad to see you're still alive. I'll try to help you guys find the leader. I'll see you later.

SAMMY
We are still trying to find a way to open the force shield. You have to reach us, Jake. And fast.

TAMMY
I'm waiting to hear back from Dim on possible solutions.

ZORN
Okay, I'll just send Jake out while we're waiting...

BECKER
Zorn, I saw this big rocket near Mason's place. If we can get Mason to fly it right at the shield, maybe we can punch through it.

ZORN
That might be the only great idea you've ever had. Jake, bring Mason to the rocket.

JAKE
Good luck, buddy.

MASON
Thanks, Jake... Whoa!

JAKE
Are you okay, Mason?

MASON
Yeah. I'm okay, Jake. I just need to rest my hands now.

BECKER
You're just full of surprises. I didn't think you'd be so
good at flying.

MASON
I used to go flying with my father, a long time ago.

ZORN
Good job, Mason. We can get to the other half of the
City now.

BECKER
Umm, Zorn? Who are these guys?

ZORN
Meet Max and Adam.

BECKER
Do you guys like to have fun?

MAX
I like to have fun.

ADAM
I also like to have fun.

MAX
Adam and I are going out for a walk.

***

DIM
Hey, Jake, Mason. It's good to see you guys again.

JAKE
What's this you've got here?

DIM
Oh, that's just my new TV. I need some help from you
guys.

MASON
What do you need, Dim?

DIM
I need someone to test this TV out to see if it's good
with my new video games.

MASON
Uh, sure... It looks pretty good to me.

DIM
Wow, I've never seen such a high score!

JAKE
Yeah, Mason's good at video games. We'll see you
around, Dim.

***

TAMMY
See that floating thing up in the sky? We think
whoever's in it is part of the war. I modified this jet
bike to get you guys up there and see who's in it.

JAKE
You can count on us, Tammy. We'll do our best to find
out who it is.

TAMMY
That's what I like to hear. Good luck, guys.

JAKE
Are you ready, Mason?

MASON
I'm always ready, Jake.

JAKE
Good. Let's do this.

DRYAN
Hey, guys. It's good to see you again. It's been a long
time.

JAKE
Hey, Dryan. It's good to see... Uh, that you're a cyborg
now.

DRYAN
Yeah, I'm a cyborg now, Jake. After I got blown up at
Baron Hax's race, some of his men put me back
together.

JAKE
Well, Tammy will be happy that one of our guys
controls this floating machine.

CAPTAIN HUNTER
[walkie talkie]
Jake, this is Captain Hunter. I need you guys to come
back to Las Vegas for a quick mission.

JAKE
Okay, Captain Hunter. We'll be there soon.

CAPTAIN HUNTER
Hey, guys. Thanks for coming back. I need you guys to
go and destroy some bombs that have been placed
around the city.

JAKE
We'll do our best. Let's go, Kig... And done. That'll be
the last time someone tries to blow up any buildings in
Vegas with bombs.

CAPTAIN HUNTER
You guys did it! The bombs are out of the picture. I'm
glad that you guys are on our side.

JAKE
Okay, Captain Hunter. We have to go back.

BECKER
Hey, Carson, look: it's Mandy. Do you want to go and
say hi to her?

CARSON
Umm... Hello, Mandy. I'm back again.

MANDY
Hey, Carson. It's good to see you guys again. How are
things?

CARSON
Umm. Good, Mandy. We came back to do another

mission for Captain Hunter.

ASHLEY
What kind of mission?

JAKE
We had to destroy some bombs in the city.

KIG
And it was easy, too.

LIZ
Wow! I think you guys are really cool. We were just
talking about you guys and how cool you are.

CARSON
You were?

MANDY
Yeah. And we'd like to go to LA with you guys.

CARSON
Uh, okay. But maybe a different time, Mandy, if that's
okay.

MANDY
Is something wrong?

CARSON
Yeah, just a little bit. We're kinda at war right now.

MANDY
Okay, Carson. Well, we'll see you later, then.

BECKER
I told you she'd like to talk to you again.

CARSON
Thanks, Becker. You really helped me out back there.

BECKER
No problem, buddy. I'm your wingman. If you need any
help with girls, I'm there for you.

CARSON
Did you just say wingman?

JAKE
Are you guys ready to go back now?

MASON
I'm ready to go back, Jake.

JAKE
Okay. Let's head back.

ZORN
Where have you been? We've been looking everywhere
for you.

DRYAN
Well, after Jake and I raced—congrats on his victory,
by the way—some guards came in and shot me a bunch
of times. Some of Baron Hax's men fought them off
and were able to help bring me back as a cyborg. It's
taken some getting used to.

ZORN
Will you be of any use to us?

DRYAN
Of course. Like I already know Vender is playing mind
games with us.

MAX
We need a man on the inside.

ZORN
And who might that be?

EMMA
I vote Jake to be our spy.

JAKE
No, I think Mason would be better.

BECKER
Umm, I was going to say Carson should be our guy.

DRYAN
What about Corbin? I think Corbin can be a good spy.

ZORN
Fine. Mason, Carson, Corbin: you're our spies. Becker,
you back them up.

BECKER
What was that?

SAMMY
That was an explosion.

TAMMY
Dang it, the City is filling with Metal Creatures and
Alloid Animals. We need to get our plans rolling, guys.

ZORN
I'm ready to move. We need to get to their nest. Jake
and Kig, you're with me.

JAKE
You got it, Zorn.

KIG
I'll drive, you shoot.

JAKE
My finger is always on the trigger.

***

LIEUTENANT RALPH
Captain Hunter, bad news: Metal Creatures and Alloid
Animals are invading LA. Orion thinks we need to give
them backup.

CAPTAIN HUNTER
Tell Lieutenant Orion to meet me at the car.

LIZ
Mandy, Ashley! I just got word that Metal Creatures
and Alloid Animals got into LA. Jake and his friends
are on their way to the nest.

ASHLEY
Should we go and help them, Mandy?

MANDY
Yes. Let's go find Captain Hunter, girls.

CAPTAIN HUNTER
Over here, ladies. I have some toys for you to help out
in this war.

MANDY
Time to catch our plane. We'll see you there.

KIG
Jake, we got a Metal Creature up there.

JAKE
I got him.

ZORN
Just try to keep up, guys. We're almost there.

MAX
Dim, what are you doing here?

DIM
I came to watch the action.

KIG
Whoa! We've got company coming this way, Jake.

JAKE
Don't worry, Kig. I got them.

ZORN
Visual on the nest. We're almost there.

KIG
Don't shoot it, Jake. Zorn needs to crack it open first.

ZORN
Jake! Fire!

JAKE
Firing!

ZORN
It looks like something is still keeping it standing. Let's
check it out. Jake, call the others.

JAKE
Tammy: this is Jake. We need you guys to come into
the nest with us.

TAMMY
[walkie talkie]
We'll be there soon.

BECKER
So this is the nest. It looks gross and scary.

ADAM
I think we should stay out here, Max.

MAX
Good plan, dude. Let us know if you need anything.

TAMMY
Don't worry, Max. We will.

KIG
Oh no, is that Vender?

JAKE
What is he doing, Kig?

KIG
I think he wants us to fight him.

JAKE
So let's go fight him.

ZORN
I was just thinking that. Let's go.

VENDER
Not so fast. Call your dumb friend Mason so he can see
what I have.

MASON
Dad.

WES
Hey, Mason. It's good to see you again, son.

MASON
It's good to see you again, too.

VENDER
Come catch me if you ever want to see your father
again.

MASON
You better not hurt my dad, Vender!

BECKER
Jake, what do we do now?

JAKE
First thing's first, we need to get Mason's dad back.

MASON
No, Jake. I'm the one who's going to free my dad. On my own.

SAMMY
No, Mason. Vender is going to kill you if you try to free your dad on your own.

MASON
I don't care about that, Sammy.

JAKE
Well, we are going to help you out anyways.

MASON
I know where Vender's hideout is. Jake, I need you to take care of his security while I find my dad.

BECKER
Good luck, Mason.

VENDER
Well well well, you made it.

JAKE
Why would you do this, Vender?

VENDER
None of your business. And since banishing you didn't

seem to work, I'll just have to kill you this time.

MASON
Dad, over here! Don't worry, I'm gonna get you out...
Jake, I freed my dad. Let's go.

KIG
See you later, Vender.

VENDER
I'll kill you guys! I'll kill you!

JAKE
Now that Mason's dad is free, we need to finish up our
business with Vender.

MASON
This is his other hideout, but where is he? Uh oh...
Jake, we've got company coming our way.

JAKE
Oh crap. Metal Creatures.

MASON
And Alloid Animals. Kill them, Jake!

CAPTAIN HUNTER
You guys need any help?

JAKE
Captain Hunter! It's good to see you again.

LIEUTENANT ORION
It's good to see you, too. I think you guys should come
in and start shooting.

JAKE
You got it, Lieutenant Orion. Sit right next to

Lieutenant Ralph, Mason.

LIEUTENANT RALPH
Captain, look out!

CAPTAIN HUNTER
Oh crap.

JAKE
Captain Hunter!

CAPTAIN HUNTER
I'm okay, Jake. My arm's just a bit hurt, that's all.

JAKE
Wait, where's Mason?

LIEUTENANT ORION
Mason is over there, Jake.

JAKE
Mason! Are you okay, buddy?

MASON
I'm just a little hurt, but I'll be fine.

LIEUTENANT RALPH
Man, what was that thing?

CAPTAIN HUNTER
That, my friend, was a rocket. They're used in battle to
blow up anything in their path.

MASON
I thought it was something else, Captain Hunter.

CAPTAIN HUNTER
Oh no, it was definitely a rocket that almost blew us up.

Keep your eyes open for more.

LIEUTENANT ORION
Let's hope that there won't be another anytime soon...

VENDER
Well well well, if it isn't Jake and Mason. And their cop friends from Vegas: Hunter, Orion, and Ralph. Jake, I've got something to tell you: Mason's dad might have gotten away, but yours is dead... Because of me. I killed your father, Jake.

JAKE
Arrrrrgh! Vender!

VENDER
I'd love to stay and chat, but I have a war to win.

CAPTAIN HUNTER
After him!

LIEUTENANT RALPH
Don't let him escape!

***

MASON
Where are we?

JAKE
I'm not sure, Mason. Kig, do you know where this is?

CREEPY VOICE
Behold!

CAPTAIN HUNTER & MASON
Ahhhhh! What was that?

CREEPY VOICE
You seek Vender? He shall be here shortly.

KIG
How do you know that?

MASON
Where is the voice coming from?

CREEPY VOICE
He always appears here.

JAKE
When will he be here?

CREEPY VOICE
When he comes down from above.

VENDER
Oh, just shut up, whoever you are!

JAKE & MASON
Vender!

CREEPY VOICE
How dare you speak to me that way! I will kill you

myself.

VENDER
Reveal yourself!

CAPTAIN HUNTER
Mack?

MACK
Yes, Dad, I was the voice. It's good to see you.

CAPTAIN HUNTER
Oh, my son, it's good to see you, too.

VENDER
Barf. I'll just kill your father like I did Jake's.

MACK
Not unless this rocket has anything to say about it.

LIEUTENANT ORION
Vender, get out of here! It's too dangerous with that
rocket!

JAKE
What?

LIEUTENANT RALPH
Orion?

MASON
What? Lieutenant Orion is on Vender's side?

LIEUTENANT ORION
That's right, I'm a backstabber. I've been working with
Vender this whole time. And now I'll finish you off so
Vender can get away and win his war.

VENDER
See you boys never.

JAKE
Quick, after them!

KIG
We can use my car. Everyone get in!

LIEUTENANT ORION
Wait, why is no one listening to me? I'm going to kill
you all!

MASON
No one's listening, you backstabber. We need to stop
Vender.

JAKE
Come on, Mason!

MASON
I'm right behind you, Jake.

***

ZORN
I really wish those guys would hurry up...

BECKER
No worries, we have this all under control. I've already
killed 22 enemies.

SAMMY
That's it? I've already killed 44. So just stop, Becker.

CARSON
Yeah, Becker, just stop.

MAX
Take that, you Metal Bear!

CARSON
Is Mason's father still safe, Zorn?

ZORN
Yes, he's fine. Now get back to fighting, Carson.

WES
I'm fine, thanks for asking.

SAMMY
Wait, who is that over there?

MAX
Is that... Vender?

VENDER
I'm here to finish the job, punks!

WES
Ahhhh!

ADAM
Go Vender! That was a nice shot.

MAX
Wait a minute, Adam. I thought you were on our side.

ADAM
No, sorry. I've always been on Vender's team. He's
going to win this war.

BECKER
And you've been shooting all our own guys!

ADAM
That's right, because I'm evil.

ZORN
Well, you picked the wrong side to turn on, Adam.

MAX
You're dead meat, Adam.

ADAM
Nooooo!

BECKER
Zorn, Max: Vender just shot Hess, too! He's escaping
on a motorcycle!

ZORN
Dang it all! This has gone too far. Jake, I hope you
know what you're doing. Stop Vender.

SAMMY
Let's finish off these Metal Creatures and Alloid
Animals, Zorn. Then we can help him out.

ZORN
You're right, Sammy.

***

VENDER
Like my sweet new ride, Jake? It's a lot better than that
car you're driving, Kig.

KIG
Take that back, you butthead. This car is a classic.

JAKE
Enough. This ends now, Vender.

VENDER
Oh, I don't think so, Jake. I'm having too much fun
making your team backstab you, and killing those who
won't be on my side.

MASON
You witch.

CORBIN
Don't forget your Powers, Jake.

VENDER
No, not the new Power! You were supposed to use that
Power to destroy Las Vegas!

JAKE
And now I will use it to stab you with my sword,
Vender.

VENDER
Ahhhhh!

KIG
Have a nice fall, Vender.

BECKER
Did you guys do it? Did you really get him?

CARSON
Would you just shut up, Becker?

JAKE
Carson, Becker, Sammy!

MASON
Zorn, Tammy, Dim!

ZORN
We saw everything. As soon as Vender's body hit the
ground, the Metal Creatures and Alloid Animals
started retreating.

SAMMY
Mason, I think you should hurry back to see your
father.

MASON
Why, Sammy? What happened to him?

BECKER
Vender shot him. And Hess, too.

MASON
I'll see you guys later. I need to go see my dad.

JAKE
See you later, buddy.

CAPTAIN HUNTER
I can't believe Orion was a traitor.

ZORN
Really? We had a traitor, too.

DIM
Who was it, Zorn?

MAX
It was Adam. I can't believe my best friend would turn
his back on us like that.

LIEUTENANT RALPH
Wow.

MASON
Dad, are you alright?

WES
Mason, I'm glad to see you. It's time for me to go.

MASON
Why is it time, Dad?

WES
It just is, son. Take care of your friends, Mason. They
need you as much as you need them.

MASON
No, Dad, you can't leave...

JAKE
I'm here for you, buddy.

SAMMY
So are the rest of us.

BECKER
So, who are you?

MACK
I'm Mack. Captain Hunter's son.

BECKER
Oh, cool.

MACK
Vender stole me away when I was really little. Right,
dad?

CAPTAIN HUNTER
Yes, son. I wasn't strong enough to save you.

MACK
It's okay, dad. I know you did your best. Just like Wes
did his best to save Mason, but couldn't.

JAKE
What?

MACK
Vender stole Mason when he was little, too.

MASON
I don't really remember, but it must be true.

CARSON
I see you're wearing diapers, Mack. That's cool. I want
to wear diapers, too.

MASON
I want to wear diapers, too. But I'm just wearing
underwear right now.

CORBIN
It's okay, Mason. You can wear diapers when you want
to.

KIG
So, what are our plans now? Any sign of our next
adventure?

JAKE
I think maybe we should take a break from being

heroes. Just for a little while.

MASON
Yeah, Jake. Our next adventure can wait.

ABOUT THE AUTHOR

Gregory Bouthiette is the author of *The Book of Adventures* and *The Book of Adventures 2*. He has two more books planned for the series. When not writing, Greg enjoys listening to music and watching videos on Youtube. You can find him on Twitter (@GregoryBouthiet) and on Youtube (The Greginator).

CATALOGUE BLUE 555